Ain't NOBODY

(A Novel)

Adrienne Thompson

Pink Cashmere Publishing, LLC

Arkansas, USA

Cover Art by A. A. Thompson (**thompson9699@gmail.com**)

Printed in the United States of America

First Printing 2015

Copyright © 2015 Adrienne Thompson

ISBN: 0988871386

ISBN-13: 978-0-9888713-8-0

Dear Lord, thank You for just being God, for blessing me with a gift, and for giving me the courage to share it. I will forever praise Your name and tell of Your goodness.

Thank you to everyone who has purchased this and any of my other books. I am so grateful for your support!!

"...for love is as strong as death, its jealousy unyielding as the grave.

It burns like blazing fire, like a mighty flame."

Song of Songs 8:6 NIV

Soundtrack

(Soundtrack playlist is available on YouTube)

"When A Woman's Fed Up" *R. Kelly*
"In My Bed" *Dru Hill*
"Me, Myself and I" *Beyoncé*
"I'm Doin' Me" *Fantasia*
"All Night Long" *Faith Evans*
"Ain't Nobody" *Chaka Khan*
"Don't Take It Personal" *Jermaine Jackson*
"Something In The Past" *Jesse Powell*
"Another Way" *Tevin Campbell*
"Say Yeah" *Kerry Thomas*
"Sumthin' Sumthin'" *Maxwell*
"Nobody's Business" *Rihanna featuring Chris Brown*
"Family Affair" *Mary J. Blige*
"Can't Let Go" *Mariah Carey*
"I Think I Love U" *Dwele*
"I Wish I Wasn't" *Heather Headley*
"Love Is A Losing Game" *Amy Winehouse*
"On And On" *Erykah Badu*
"I'm For Real" *Howard Hewett*
"I Wanna Know" *Joe*
"Me and Mr. Jones" *Amy Winehouse*
"The First Night" *Monica*
"Get It Together" *702*
"Gettin' In the Way" *Jill Scott*
"I Can't Help The Way I Feel" *Repunza*
"Remember The Time" *Michael Jackson*
"Tha Crossroads" *Bone Thugs n Harmony*
"Can We Talk" *Tevin Campbell*
"Stop The World" *Maxwell*

Prologue

Sometimes a woman's just had enough. No matter how she may feel about a man. No matter how much she loves him and wants to be with him, there's always that one, teeny tiny little straw—the *last* straw. It usually pops up after she's done all she can humanly possibly do to make things work. She's cooked for him, cleaned for him, praised him, had sex with him, ignored his annoying ways, and yet, she still finds herself holding the short end of the stick.

As I sat there on the side of Quincy's bed, the last straw flew in through the bedroom window and landed right on my camel's back. Quincy, my fiancé and the love of my life, was in the shower whistling. He was whistling like he didn't have a care in the world. He was whistling like I wasn't thirty-seven and kicking the hell out of forty. He was whistling like I wasn't unmarried and childless. Like we hadn't been engaged for five years. *Five years.* He was whistling like he hadn't refused to set a wedding date. Like my biological clock wasn't ticking as loud as a time bomb.

I'd been with Quincy Wright for eight years. I'd been his lover and friend. I'd bent over backwards, neglected my own needs, and done all I could do to be a good woman. I wanted a husband and I wanted children and he knew it. We'd discussed it *at length*. And what was his response? His black behind was in the shower whistling. That was it, and whether he knew it or not, it was over. O-V-E-R.

1

"When A Woman's Fed Up"

"Are you gonna answer that?" Gwin asked.

I shook my head and pressed the button on my cell phone to reject the call. "Nope."

Gwin sighed. "Okay, it's been three weeks. Haven't you punished him enough?"

"Humph, three weeks versus eight years? I think not."

"Alex, you act like he *made* you stay with him for eight years. That was *your* choice." My best friend was always the voice of reason in my life, and she was right. But so was I.

"I know that, but that doesn't mean I have to waste another eight years on him. Quincy and I are just not on the same page. We're not even in the same book."

"I know you want a family, but is this the way to get it? Are you just gonna punish him until he gives in?"

I wriggled my nose. Why did my nose always choose to itch when I was getting my nails done? "No, I'm done with him. I told you, he was whistling."

She rolled her eyes. "And what does that mean again?"

"It means he'll never marry me. He's happy and satisfied with the way things are, and he's not compelled to change them."

"And you got all of that from a whistle?"

I shook my head. "Not just a whistle. Look, I've known this stuff for a while. There have been signs all over the place, but I chose to ignore them. I'm tired of ignoring them now, and I'm tired of Quincy."

"What are you gonna do then?"

I shrugged. "I was gonna take him to Rio for his birthday, but now I think I'll just go by myself and find someone to help me forget about Quincy. Unless you wanna come with me."

Gwin shook her head. "Girl, I'd love to go, but Matt is not gonna let me go to the land of fun and sex without him." Gwin was short and round with a medium brown complexion and a pixie haircut. She wore trendy, rectangular eyeglasses and had been married since the beginning of time.

"See, that's what I'm saying. All I want is for someone to care about my comings and goings."

"Quincy cares."

"Whatever."

"Eight years is a lot to throw away."

"Tell Quincy that."

"Alex, you didn't even tell him why you stopped seeing him. Don't you owe him that much?"

I shrugged again.

"Look, you're gonna have to talk to him. If he keeps calling me, my husband's gonna swear we're having an affair."

As if on cue, my phone rang. I looked at Gwin and said, "Okay." Then I carefully hit the button on my phone and cradled it in my free hand. "Hello, Quincy? Yeah, you need to stop calling Gwin. Her husband is getting upset." I ended the call and slipped my phone into my purse. "There," I said to Gwin.

Gwin's eyes were wide as she said, "That is not what I meant."

I feigned innocence. "Well, what did you mean?"

"Never mind."

She didn't bring up Quincy again that day. Instead, she went about engaging in her usual, favorite pastime—talking about any and every one we knew. Gwin was an Olympic-caliber gossiper.

***

I was sitting in my mother's living room enjoying our weekly visit when she decided to ruin it for me.

"He calls me every day. Sounds like he's crying half the time," she said out of the blue.

"Who?" I asked as I picked up a *People* magazine from the coffee table and studied the cover like I was going to be quizzed on it later.

"You know who. When you gon' make up with him?"

"I'm not. We're over."

Mama leaned forward in her recliner and shook her finger at me. "A man is hard to come by—especially one with a job. He ain't got no kids and he's got his own place. I don't know what else you could want, Alex."

I turned my head towards the TV, which was playing a Tyler Perry DVD with the volume muted. "Commitment."

"Ain't y'all engaged?"

"Yes, but if I leave it up to Quincy, we'll be engaged forever. I mean, by the time you were my age, you'd already been married twice. Farrah's younger than me, and she's already been married *and* divorced. And look at Gwin. She's been married forever. I just want my chance to have a family."

Mama frowned. "Well, hell, ain't none of that worth bragging about. Farrah's divorced, I've been married twice, and Gwin's husband won't even go to church with her. What kind of marriage is that? I don't know what you think marriage is, but let me be the first to tell you, it ain't no fairy tale. It's a bunch of work. Sometimes it's worth the trouble, and sometimes it's not. But one thing's for sure, you ain't gone get no closer to marrying the man by quitting him. That just don't make no sense to me."

I sighed. "Mama, I really don't want to discuss this." I pointed to the TV. "Which one is this? *I Can Do Bad All By Myself?*"

"Naw, *Diary of a Mad Black Woman*. Alex, you're making a mistake."

Before I could answer, I heard the front door open and close and seconds later, my younger sister, Farrah, walked in wearing tight jeans and a tank top. She was six years my junior, and she was gorgeous. She was petite with the smoothest brown skin, and I'd literally kill for her body. She'd already had one husband, two kids, and two baby daddies, but she looked like she was still in high school.

"Hey, y'all," she said as she plopped down on the sofa next to me. "Where the kids?"

"They in the family room playing one of those video games," Mama said.

"Well, can they stay here tonight? I got some stuff I need to do," Farrah asked.

"*Someone* you need to do," I said under my breath.

"I heard that, Alex. Don't hate on me just because you ain't got no man. Oh, that's right, you had one but you threw him away," Farrah countered.

"You have no idea what you're talking about. Why don't you worry about raising your kids, and stop leaving them on Mama all the time?" I said through my teeth.

"That's enough!" Mama shouted.

We were all startled by the ringing of the doorbell.

"I'll get it," I said. I cut my eyes at Farrah as I headed to the front door. Mama shook her head as I passed by her. I opened the door and wanted to scream. Mama had planned this, and I knew it. Standing on the other side of the door was Quincy.

"Mama! I think you have company!" I yelled as Quincy stood there and stared at me.

"No, I don't. That's *your* company," she called back.

I rolled my eyes and let out an exasperated sigh. "I don't know why Mama did this. What is it, Q?"

He smiled. "You're the only person who calls me that, you know?"

"Then I'll stop."

He dropped the smile and his shoulders. Quincy Wright was a nice-looking man. He was tall and husky with pale brown skin. His moustache and goatee were always neatly trimmed as was his thick hair, and he always smelled like Armani Code. He looked so good standing there in his business suit, I had to fight to stay in character. Oh, yeah. Did I mention he's a lawyer and a successful one, at that? Yeah, I know.

"Alex, why won't you talk to me?" he asked.

"Because I'm done, Quincy."

"Can you tell me exactly what I've done to deserve this?"

I glanced behind me. I really didn't want Farrah and Mama any deeper in my business than they already were. "Let's step outside." I closed the door and sat down on one of the resin chairs on Mama's porch. Quincy sat down beside me. "Quincy, do you love me, I mean *really* love me?"

"Of course I do. You know that."

"And you like being with me?"

He nodded. "Yes."

"Then why won't you marry me?"

He smiled. "Baby, we're engaged."

"I know that, but when are we getting married? This ring is not enough for me anymore," I said as I held up my left hand. "I need a date."

"You know I'm trying to get my practice off the ground. I work crazy hours. It's not time, yet."

I stood and folded my arms over my chest. "Then it will never be time. You have your own law firm. You'll always work crazy hours."

"I'm going to marry you, Alex. I just need time to pull things together. I want everything to be right."

"Q, you have a house, a nice car, a growing business, and let's not forget that I happen to make a decent living. Things *are* right."

Quincy stood and cupped my face in his hands. "I just need more time, baby," he said softly.

I dropped my eyes. "No. I'm running out of time. I want a family. I'm done waiting."

He sighed. "Okay."

I looked up at him. "Okay, what?"

"Okay, let's do it. I don't want to lose you."

"Don't do this unless you want to, Quincy."

He kissed me softly. "I really want to. We can do it as soon as possible. No more waiting."

I smiled. "If we do it next weekend, the trip to Brazil can be our honeymoon."

He hugged me. "Then next weekend it is."

Farrah walked out onto the porch. "Y'all made up? How nice."

I held onto Quincy and closed my eyes. *Hater*, I thought.

2

"In My Bed"

I sat in my car in the middle of Houston rush hour traffic and groaned. I really needed to get to Quincy's house to get my phone. I'd forgotten it when I left that morning. I'd stopped by my mother's house and tried calling it but I'd left it on vibrate, so I was sure Quincy couldn't hear it, and he wasn't answering his phone, so he couldn't bring it to me, and I *needed* my phone. How was I to plan a spur of the moment wedding without it? I needed to be at the bakery to approve the cake design in an hour, and after that, I had a day filled with wedding-planning scheduled. At the rate the traffic was going, I'd be behind schedule the entire day.

I inched and inched along until, thirty minutes later, I made it to the house that would become my home in just a few days as I was planning to rent my own home out. His car was in the driveway. *Maybe he's asleep*, I thought. *I guess I wore him out.* I grinned at the thought of the bedroom workout we'd had earlier that morning. I unlocked the door with my key and walked in. Q's house always smelled like a mixture of cherries and vanilla—his two favorite incense fragrances.

I walked through his spacious living room with its sleek black furniture and plush beige carpet. I walked towards the hall that led to his bedroom and stopped dead in my tracks. I could hear Quincy talking. Was it talking or moaning?

Moaning?

MOANING?!

I stood there and listened. I wanted to turn and leave or run in there and kick his tail, but I was frozen. I just stood there and listened. It wasn't long before his moans were joined by a more feminine set of moans. *Leave, Alex. Just leave,* my mind repeated. I tried, but I couldn't. I was… paralyzed. The tears began to fall, and I just stood there. My heart began to crack, and still, I stood there.

The moaning finally ended as did the squeaking of the mattress. I heard them talking, and yet I still stood there. Though I begged my feet to move, they wouldn't, or maybe they couldn't.

She was the first to emerge from the bedroom. She was wearing his oversized Texas Southern t-shirt, and she was glowing. She entered the hallway, saw me, and a look of shock spread across her face. "Alex?!" she shrieked.

"What?!" I heard Quincy say. And then he appeared in the hallway wearing the same boxers I'd left him in that morning. I spun on my heels and ran out of the house. My feet were finally working again, thank God. As I ran to my car, I could hear Quincy yelling behind me, "Alex! Baby, wait! Wait!"

I fumbled with the button on my key fob, and then dropped my keys. "Damn!" I screamed.

He caught up with me and grabbed my arm. "Baby, listen."

I snatched away from him and fell to my knees to pick up my keys. Suddenly, I felt light-headed and started heaving. Before I realized what was happening, I'd vomited right there in his driveway. What he'd done, what *they'd* done, had literally made me sick.

"Baby, you all right?" he asked as I stood to my feet.

"Quincy, get away from me!" I unlocked the door and tried to open it, but he pushed it shut.

"Alex, listen. Let me explain."

"Listen to what? How exactly can you explain this? What happened, Q? Did you trip and fall right in between my sister's legs?!" I screamed.

"I'm sorry. It was a mistake. I love you, Alex. I really do."

"You love me?! Go to hell, Quincy. *Please* go to hell. I expect as much from her sorry tail, but you?"

"He don't think I'm sorry," Farrah said. She was perched on the front steps of Quincy's house, still sporting nothing but his t-shirt.

"Shut up, girl!" Quincy shouted at her.

I glared at my sister. "You know what, Farrah? You can take a one-way trip to Sheol, too." I turned back to Quincy. "MOVE!" My voice sounded different—not like my own, but like someone else's. It startled Quincy, and he looked a little frightened as he backed away from my car. I climbed in, and the smell of the puke on my blouse overwhelmed me. I let my windows down, pulled the shirt over my head, and threw it out onto the driveway. I started the car and revved the engine. Everything in me wanted to run over Quincy. Visions of him lying crumpled in his driveway with tire tracks tattooed into the side of his face swirled around in my head.

I stared at him as I gunned the engine over and over again. But fortunately, or maybe unfortunately, a little bit of sanity kicked in and I backed out of the driveway. I cried as I rode home wearing only my bra and jeans. I'm sure I garnered a lot of curious looks from my fellow motorists, but I just didn't care.

***

I lay in my bed on the morning of what was to be my wedding day and stared at the ceiling. I sighed. I'd been in that bed since the fateful day on which my world fell apart, and the only thoughts running through my head were: *I hate Quincy Wright, and I wish he'd die and go to hell.*

Harsh, I know, but it was honestly how I felt. I also hated my sister. I hated her, and if she slid down a slippery slope into the lake of fire, I wouldn't have been all that upset. Hell, who was I kidding? Her demise would be cause for celebration. A big celebration with a cake and balloons and a Mariachi band and some damn clowns, too.

My landline and cell phone took turns ringing. It was Quincy, and I was tired of him. I was so very tired of him that I wished he would literally disappear. I closed my eyes and tried to block out the ringing, but his ignorant behind kept right on marathon calling.

I sat up on the side of the bed and screamed, then I snatched the cordless phone from the night stand and shouted into it, "WHAT DO YOU WANT, Q?!"

"Alex, I miss you, baby. Please, please talk to me. What I did was a mistake. I was just so stressed about the wedding and you were putting all this pressure on me and I need you. *I'm so sorry*," he said, his words coming out in a rush.

I gripped the phone tightly and bit down on my bottom lip. "Quincy Terrell Wright, listen and listen good, because I don't want you to miss a single word. I do not give a hell what you have to say or how you feel. There is nothing in any language you can say to explain why you had sex with my sister days before our wedding. Stop calling me like a stupid fool, *please*. I hope she gave you a VD you disgusting, amoral pig!"

After I hung up, I called and had both of my numbers changed. Afterwards I called the only two people that mattered to me, Gwin and my mother, and gave them my new numbers. Both of them got off the phone pretty quickly. I don't think either of them knew what to say since they'd both been Quincy's cheerleaders. Mama sounded so worried, and I hated she was thrown into the middle of this mess. I hated that Farrah was such a slut and had been a source of stress for Mama for so many years. She was truly a bad seed.

I shook my head as I headed to the bathroom and got a glimpse of my reflection in the mirror above the sink. I looked like a pure hot mess. I threaded my fingers through my micro braids and fought back bitter tears. I'd had my hair braided especially for our trip to Brazil. We were supposed to fly out of Houston that very evening. *So much money wasted.* But the money was nothing compared to the time I'd wasted. Eight years of my life were gone, and I could never get them back. *Never.*

I balled up my fists and beat them against the mirror as my hatred for my man and my sister began to brim over again. "Why?!" I screamed. "Why?! Why?! Why?!" The glass began to crack beneath my blows, but that didn't stop me. I didn't even stop when I felt the glass penetrate my hands. I needed this. I needed a release. I needed to punish *something.*

I'd cut up all of his pictures, destroyed every card he'd given me, shredded every letter or note. I'd erased his text messages and emails, blocked him on Facebook and Twitter. What was left? What else could I do besides abuse this mirror? I honestly couldn't think of anything else I could do to make me feel better other than driving my car through the big picture window in his living room and not stopping until I ran his cheating, lying tail over repeatedly. Then I'd drag his limp body down I45, all the way to Dallas where his body would finally dislodge from beneath my Yukon and be flattened by an eighteen-wheeler.

But I couldn't do that. He wasn't worth the jail time. I'd had the same thoughts about Farrah, but she was worth even less than

Quincy, and that's pretty darn cheap. I caught sight of my bloody hands and stopped. Hurting myself was stupid. Hadn't they already hurt me enough? As I wiped my hands with a soft towel, I told myself that I needed to find something to do, something to take my mind off of them and what they'd done to me. As I walked back into my bedroom, it hit me.

I walked swiftly to my closet, grabbed a couple of suitcases, and began to pack. I was going to Rio. I was going to Rio and I was going to find one of those fine Brazilian men and have more anonymous sex than I could even imagine. I was going to go to Rio and push Quincy Wright and Farrah House as far out of my brain as possible. Damn them.

3

Me, Myself and I

I spent most of the 14-hour, non-stop flight to Rio de Janeiro thinking about the two people I was trying to forget. Farrah and Quincy stayed on my mind no matter how hard I tried to block them out.

Farrah was my baby sister, and other than my half-brother, who was my father's child from his second marriage, she was my only sibling. I never understood why she hated me, but she always had. Gwin always said Farrah was jealous of me, but I never believed it. Farrah was always so beautiful, and all the things I wanted, she'd already had. She had two wonderful children—Tia and Darnell, Jr. She was single, but at least she'd been married once. Why would she be jealous of me?

Maybe it was my career she envied. Farrah never finished college. I graduated Summa Cum Laude from Baylor University with a degree in Business Management, and up until four years ago, I was VP of Marketing for Gracious Beauty Cosmetics. I was making six figures and rubbing elbows with members of Houston's high society, but I was also miserable and unfulfilled. I prayed for happiness in that job but couldn't find it.

I did a lot of soul-searching and ended up returning to my first love, writing. I had always loved writing poetry and short stories and had often been complimented on my writing skills. So I decided to take another stab at it, hoping that it would at least serve as a stress-reliever. The first story I wrote turned into a full-fledged novel. I sent my manuscript out to several publishing companies, only to be rejected time and time again.

Frustrated, but determined to succeed, I quit my job, cashed in my 401K, and invested in my future. I self-published my book. Now, three years and a series of best-selling books later, it seemed that I made the right decision. Readers had a great appreciation for my take on the dating game. The *Diva Chronicles* was a series of stories about the adventures of a quartet of plus-sized beauties. It was my version of a black, full-figured *Sex and the City*. My books were so popular, I eventually signed with an agent and was picked up by a publishing company. Now the stories of Nadine, Allison, India, and Denise were being turned into a TV miniseries. I was loving my life and my career, and with Quincy by my side, I didn't think things could get any better.

I loved Quincy. I really did. I'd dated before in high school and college and even in grad school, but I'd never said "I love you" until Quincy. I met him during Farrah's divorce. He was her lawyer, and since her husband had taken their only car when he left, I was her only ride to Quincy's office. It wasn't until after her divorce was finalized that he asked me out. He was handsome and charming, and we hit it off right away. Quincy was smart and confident, and he wasn't half-bad in bed either. So I gave him a quick "yes" when he asked if we could see each other exclusively. I was very excited when we exchanged keys a year later. To me, when a man gives you his key, it means he has nothing to hide and that he trusts you. Of course I was elated when Quincy proposed. But that was then, and this is now. Yes, I was once a very happy and contented woman, but in one act, Farrah and Quincy destroyed that happiness.

One act.

Had it really been one time, or had they been seeing each other for years? After all, Quincy was Farrah's lawyer before I met him. Just how long had I been the blind fool in this equation?

I shut my eyes and shook my head. *Forget them.* They weren't worth the brain cells it took to think about them, let alone the spit it took to cuss them. I put on my headphones, turned on my MP3 player, closed my eyes, and let Maxwell croon me the rest of the way to Brazil.

4

"I'm Doin' Me"

After an extremely long flight, I attempted to shake the stiffness from my joints as I made my way through the bustling terminal with my luggage. Carnival was beginning, and Rio would soon be filled to capacity with tourists, spectators, and participants. I had to stand in an unbearably long line to get immigration clearance and have my passport checked, but from what I'd always heard, Rio would definitely be worth the trouble.

I was thankful that the Caesar Park Hotel provided a shuttle service from the airport. I breathed a sigh of relief when I finally made it outside Rio de Janeiro–Galeão International Airport and climbed into the van where I was joined by three couples. But suddenly it stung to be alone. This was supposed to be my honeymoon trip. I should have been sitting next to Quincy. As I watched the couples smile and chat with one another, I felt tears sting my eyes. I dug around in my oversized purse and fished out my sunglasses. Those people were happy, and there was no need in my heartache spoiling their bliss. *Maybe I shouldn't have come. Maybe this was a bad idea. Damn.*

***

I felt a little better when I made it to my room. From my balcony, I had a perfect view of Guanabar Bay and Ipanema Beach, which was teeming with bikini-clad bodies. I'd packed my one-piece, but judging from the toned bodies on that beach, I doubted I'd be wearing it.

I walked back into the room and called Gwin and my mother to let them know I'd made it safely. Then I sat on the side of the bed and took in my plush surroundings. The room was beautiful, decorated in soothing earth tones. The king-sized bed was comfortable, to say the least, and the huge, flat-screen TV was even nicer than the one in my living room at home.

I was in paradise, and the sun was shining brightly. I had a bunch of money, and the beach was lined with shops and restaurants. The hotel even had a rooftop pool. But all I could do was sit there with my thoughts and my disappointment and my pain. So, I sat there in my beautiful suite and cried. I cried the afternoon away, and then I went to bed.

The next morning I pulled myself together. I was in Rio. *Rio!* How many big girls from Texas could say that? So, first thing the next morning, I headed to the hotel's restaurant and overloaded on the breakfast buffet. I told myself it was okay to pig out since I'd missed dinner the previous night. Afterwards, I headed to my massage appointment, and after that, I'd get in a little shopping. Then dinner at a restaurant one of the front desk clerks had recommended.

I walked into the massage parlor and was ushered into a room where I undressed and wrapped a wonderfully soft cloth around my thick body. I lay on the thin table, nervously hoping that a woman would be providing my massage. Sure, I'd come to Rio with hopes of engaging in lots of anonymous sex, but I really didn't want a man to see my 5'5" and 216 pounds of naked flesh. Really, I didn't. But, of course, when the door to the room finally creaked open, it was a heavily-accented male voice that greeted me.

"How are you today, Miss?" he asked.

I sat up on the table, poised to request a female masseuse, and dang near fell off of it. This dude was fine, and when I say fine, I mean, *FINE*—in all caps. The kind of fine that makes you blink and rub your eyes and wonder if you're dreaming. He was tall, maybe a little more than six feet, and muscular, with biceps that bulged through the sleeves of his crisp, white polo shirt, and the white chinos he wore fit him perfectly. His skin was medium-brown with ruddy undertones. It was a unique skin color that reminded me of the brown skin characteristic of persons of Middle Eastern descent— odd, difficult to describe, but beautiful. His amber eyes were wrapped in lashes so dark and thick, he almost appeared to be wearing eyeliner. His thick, curly hair was dark brown with blond highlights and fell to his shoulders. I knew many a sister who'd be willing to pay top dollar for hair like his, and I couldn't help imagining getting my fingers tangled in it. I figured he was a mixture of more than one race—maybe even more than two.

This man was absolutely gorgeous, and when he flashed me his thousand-watt smile, I almost peed on myself. He was so striking that I forgot to request a female masseuse. Hell, for a second there, I forgot my own name. I just sat there holding the cloth over my breasts and staring at him with my mouth hung open, darn near drooling. Lord-have-mercy!

His smile diminished. "Ah, como vai?"

I stared at him until my good sense kicked back in. "Oh, no. I don't speak Portuguese. I'm… I'm American."

He smiled again. "Okay, lie down, and we can begin?"

I nodded and resumed my former position on the table. He lowered the cloth to expose my back, and when his hands met my skin, I felt a heat spread through my body, all the way down to my toes. *Down, girl.* He gently rubbed oil on my back, and my eyes rolled up into my head. Boy, was he good with his hands. Before I knew it, I'd let out a soft moan. I hoped he didn't hear me.

"Where in United States are you from?" he asked as the session drew to a close.

"Texas."

"Ah, George Bush."

I laughed. "I guess we *are* known for him, now."

"And Beyoncé."

I chuckled. "Yeah."

He kneaded the muscles in my left leg. "You have beautiful skin."

You have beautiful everything. "Um, thank you."

"Are you here for Carnival?"

I nodded. "Yes. I've wanted to come for years. Finally got the chance."

He rubbed my shoulders. "I hope that you and your husband enjoy Carnival," he whispered in my ear.

My body tingled in places I didn't even know existed. "Thank you," I replied. My mind screamed: *Tell him you ain't got no husband, fool!*

"You're so tense. You should come back tomorrow, same time. Ask for me, Victor. What is your name?"

"Alexandria."

"Beautiful name. Tomorrow, then."

I smiled shyly. "Okay."

If they'd hired Victor to make more money from those massages, they'd definitely made a wise choice. Victor was so fine and his hands felt so good; I was seriously considering getting several massages a day during my stay.

* * *

That evening, I had dinner on my balcony. To make up for my gluttonous breakfast, I had a salad and some fruit. I smiled at the scenery below. The gorgeous white sand of the beach now held a sparser crowd, and the moon reflected on the ocean beautifully. Rio is a gorgeous place. A huge metropolis set against a backdrop of pure paradise. It is a perfect place for love and for lovers. *Love.* I shook my head. No sense in going there. I was thankful when my cell phone rang. My best friend had just saved me from another dive into depression.

"Hello?" I said.

"Hey, girl! You on the beach sipping some exotic cocktail?" Gwin asked excitedly.

"Naw, girl. I'm on the balcony of my room having dinner."

"Dinner? Isn't it kinda late?"

"That's how they do it here."

"So, tell me. Is it as beautiful as I've seen in the movies and on TV?"

"*More beautiful.* The beach is always full of people, gorgeous people. Oh, and I got a massage earlier today."

"Ooooh! I bet you're all relaxed now."

"Well, actually, the masseur, Victor, asked me to come back tomorrow. He said I'm still pretty tense."

"Victor? You let a man give you a massage?"

"I let a fine-tail man give me a massage. Girl, he is so fine, I might have to bring him home with me!"

Gwin laughed. "Well, at least take his picture. I'm married, but I can look."

I laughed. "I'll do my best."

"Oh, and take some pictures of the beach, too."

"Okay."

"I'll let you go. Bye, girl."

"Bye, Gwin."

I hung up and turned my attention back to the beach. Growing up, I was always the chubby girl, and I'd always had low self-esteem. It had taken me years to feel good about myself and my body. Finding out about Farrah and Quincy—the one person I truly believed loved me for me—had wounded my self-confidence. After all, Farrah and I were complete opposites physically. Maybe Quincy had been attracted to Farrah all along. Why wouldn't he be?

I sighed. As bad as I wanted to, there was just no way I was going to put on my bathing suit and walk out onto that beach amongst those hard bodies. No way at all.

5

Around eleven the next morning, I walked into the massage parlor and asked for Victor. 11:00 AM in Brazil is 9:00 AM in Texas. Not much of a difference, but since I was self-employed and accustomed to sleeping in every morning, I felt it. I was tired, but I wanted the massage if for no other reason than to see Victor again. For that, I would've crawled out of bed at 2:00 AM during the new moon phase and trekked across the city barefoot *and* naked. He was just that fine.

I stood and waited as the girl behind the desk eyed me. You almost would've thought she was Victor's woman and I had confessed my undying love for him or something. I looked away from her and tapped my foot. *I sure hope I'm not gonna get jumped on over a masseur. He ain't fine enough to fight over,* I thought.

I was about to say "forget it" and leave when Victor finally appeared, escorting a tall blond to the parlor exit. She was glowing like she'd had the massage of a lifetime. The girl behind the desk rolled her eyes and said something in Portuguese, and judging from the way Victor's head snapped in my direction, I assumed she'd announced my presence. As he walked in my direction, I swear I could hear The Isley Brothers' "Between the Sheets" playing in my head.

He smiled warmly. "Alexandria!" He grabbed my hands and kissed me on each cheek—fine moustache stubble scratched my skin. Man, he smelled good! My knees buckled a little. "Follow me," he said. I glanced at the girl behind the desk and noticed her glaring at us as we left.

I followed Victor to a small room at the end of the hallway and watched as he closed the door behind us. "May I?" he asked.

I was confused until he gently tugged at the belt of my robe. I looked down at the belt and then back up at him. His eyes burned into mine, and I really believe he hypnotized me or something. Because before I even realized it, I was nodding in agreement. Victor began to slowly untie the belt; then he stopped. "Will your husband care if I see your body?" he asked.

"I'm not married," I answered softly.

He raised his eyebrows. "Boyfriend?"

I shook my head. "No."

He leaned closer to me and whispered, "Good."

He untied the belt, opened my robe, eyed my nakedness from head to toe, and said, "Beautiful."

I blushed.

I stared at him as he peeled the robe off of me. "No cloth today, yeah?" he said.

I nodded.

I lay on the table, suddenly ashamed of my body again. I closed my eyes as Victor's oiled hands glided over my skin, kneading and caressing me. I sighed inwardly. Victor was an absolute genius with his hands, and I felt like I was in Heaven. All thoughts of Farrah and Quincy had melted away. I felt totally at ease and totally free.

"Alexandria, you are so beautiful," Victor whispered.

"Thank you," I said.

The massage lasted for a long while—much longer than the allotted 45 minutes. Victor took his time and massaged every inch of my skin, and his touch was simply divine. I kept my eyes closed and pretended he was my lover. I pretended I *had* a lover. I felt tears flood my eyes as reality assaulted my mind. Before I knew it, I was sobbing audibly. Victor wrapped his arms around me and leaned against my body. He didn't say a word, and I was glad for the silence and the comfort. Softly, gently he kissed my back, my arms, and then he turned my face and kissed my lips. And I let him. I don't know why I let him, but I know it felt good. Somehow, it felt right. Unfortunately, though, we were interrupted by a knock at the door.

"I'm sorry. Excuse me," Victor said softly.

I reached down, grabbed a cloth, and covered my body as Victor answered the door. When he stepped outside the room, I wiped my face and climbed off of the table. A few seconds later, Victor returned with an apologetic look on his face. "My next appointment has arrived."

I nodded, picked up my robe, and wrapped it around my body. Victor grabbed my hand as I began to tie the belt. "Are you feeling, ah… better?" he asked.

I offered him a weak smile. "Yes."

He caressed my cheek. "You are too beautiful for tears."

My smile widened.

He leaned in and kissed my cheek. "What are you doing tonight?"

I shrugged. "Nothing."

"I take you to see Rio?"

Surprised, I said, "Oh, okay. Sure."

"Your room number?"

I didn't know Victor. All I knew was he was handsome and he had the hands of a magician, but the last thing I wanted to do was sit up in that room alone. To that end, I said, "1504."

"Okay, eight o'clock." He kissed my other cheek, let his hand slide down my back and rest on my behind. "Tchau."

"Tchau," I said.

He walked me all the way to the exit door and as I made my way to my room, I could still feel his embrace and the sensation of his lips on my skin.

***

At 8:00 P.M., I was sitting in my suite, nervously watching the door. Coupled with the nervousness, an excitement was bubbling inside of me like a cauldron. None of this made sense. I didn't even know Victor's last name, and for all I knew he was some crazed, maniacal, Brazilian serial killer who preyed on lonely, fat, unsuspecting American women. But I liked him and I liked looking at him and I liked his touch. He was smooth and skilled in much more than massage therapy—I was sure of that. And I'd be lying if I said I didn't want to find out about his other skills.

I glanced at my watch. 8:02. *He's not coming.* That thought was followed by the sting of tears. I fought them back, but I was still hurt. *Why are you upset?* I asked myself. *You don't even know this man.*

At 8:05, I walked out onto the balcony and looked at Ipanema Beach. *Why did you come here? What did you think would happen? This place is for lovers and people having fun. You're all alone in paradise. Go home.*

That last voice was pretty convincing—so convincing that I actually found myself pulling my suitcase from the closet and was just about to pack when I heard a knock at the door. My heart jumped. *Calm down. You don't even know if it's him.*

I peered through the peep hole. It *was* Victor, and he looked *good*. My hand trembled as I reached for the doorknob. I pulled my hand back, closed my eyes, and took a deep breath. When I reached for the knob again, my hand was much steadier. I opened it and wordlessly let him into the room. He was wearing a white suit with a black shirt partially unbuttoned to show off his toned chest, and his hair was pulled back into a ponytail. His bright smile quickly dissipated once he got a good look at my face. I'd never been very good at hiding my emotions. He glanced over at the bed and noticed my suitcase.

"Are you leaving?" he asked.

I shrugged. "I have no idea what I'm doing." I slumped onto the bed and clasped my hands in my lap.

Victor took a seat next to me on the bed. "Why did you come to Rio? For Carnival, yeah?"

I sighed as I fixed my eyes on the floor. "This was supposed to be my honeymoon."

Victor placed a hand on my shoulder. "He broke your heart?"

I looked up at him, and the sympathetic expression covering his handsome face brought my hard-fought tears back to the surface. Victor wrapped his arms around me, and I leaned against him, resting my head on his chest. I cried for a few minutes as he held me and gently rubbed his hand up and down my arm.

"Thank you for letting me cry... *again*," I said softly.

He smiled. "I want to make you smile. You will let me do that?"

I wiped my cheeks. "Yes, okay."

He closed his eyes, gently pressed his forehead against mine, and kissed me tenderly on the lips. I closed my eyes as he kissed me again and again. And when he unbuttoned my white blouse and un-tucked it from my white peasant skirt, I didn't stop him. Nor did I stop him when he gently pushed me until my back rested on the soft bed and continued to undress me. He unbuckled my sandals and kissed all ten of my toes, one-by-one. He kissed and caressed my bare legs, my jiggly thighs, my soft stomach, and then I heard him say, "Are you smiling, Alexandria?"

"No," I replied. I was too busy holding my breath to smile.

"No?" he whispered. He kissed and caressed and awakened places on my body that had been in hibernation for a long time. And when he'd literally driven me up a wall, he quizzed me again. "Are you smiling?"

"Uh... uh..." was all I managed to say. I was unable to form even the simplest coherent sentence or phrase.

"Still more work for me?"

I bit down on my lip, grunted softly.

"The walls are sound proof," he said.

Well, he shouldn't have told me *that*.

He worked his way up and down my body, exploring it as if it were a newly discovered land. But then again, I guess that's exactly what I was to him. Then he stopped and stood from the bed, making a show of undressing for me, and I definitely enjoyed every single nanosecond of it. If Adonis was real, Victor was most assuredly a bronzed carbon copy of him. There was absolutely no part of his body that I did not admire. He was a sight to behold. *Lord, have mercy!*

He turned the bedside radio on, and soft bossa nova music began to fill the room. With anticipation threatening to overtake me, he finally rejoined me in the bed. I'd spent the last eight years of my life with one man—*Quincy*. Before him, I'd been intimate with a handful of guys, but none of them, and I mean *none of them*, including Quincy, had ever made me feel the way Victor I-don't-even-know-his-last-name made me feel. When he was done with me, I felt like I'd just run a mile in a pair of six-inch heels. I was exhausted, spent, and exhilarated all at the same time. Shoot, he made me want to sing Chaka Khan's "Ain't Nobody" out loud for the world to hear, and I can't sing a lick.

As I lay there in the bed staring at the ceiling and trying to catch my breath, Victor said, "Where's that smile?"

6

"Ain't Nobody"

Early the next morning, I awakened with my head resting on Victor's chest, tempted to pinch myself. What that man had done to me literally made my toes curl. I felt tingly from head to toe, like I'd been dipped in a vat of something cool and airy. I felt... *alive,* and I loved that feeling. I could've lain in his arms for every second of what was left of my life, and it still wouldn't have been enough. He was truly a fantasy come true.

"Bom dia... good morning," he said, breaking into my thoughts.

I smiled. "Good morning."

He kissed my forehead. "I have work this morning, but I still want to show you Rio. Tonight? Eight o'clock?"

I smiled again. "Okay."

Victor peered down at my face, his own face framed by a mass of curls. "Ah, the smile. There it is." He climbed out of bed, leaned over, and pressed a soft kiss to my lips.

I pulled the sheet over my body and watched as he dressed in the previous night's clothes. After he slipped on his shoes, he walked back over to the bed and planted yet another kiss on my lips. I reached up and wrapped my arms around his neck.

"Mm, I must go," he said.

"Okay, I'll see you tonight," I said softly.

"Tchau," he said as he headed to the door.

"Tchau," I replied.

Victor reached the door and hesitated. "I will be late," he said as he turned and looked at me. I gave him a confused look, but when he began to shed his clothes, I understood what he'd meant. *Well, all right then*, I thought. Seconds later, he rejoined me in the bed, and I thoroughly enjoyed making him late for work.

***

That afternoon, after a long, relaxing bath, I put on my black, one-piece swimsuit and wrapped a colorful sarong around my waist. I stepped into a pair of flip-flops and smiled as I left the hotel and walked out onto the white sands of Ipanema Beach, swaying my hips to a rhythm in my head. I bought a huge, floppy straw hat from one of the vendors on the beach and rented a beach chair from a different vendor. I got myself some delicious coconut water and soon settled down in the chair. Then I pulled out my phone and took a few pictures of the beach, the people, and the ocean as the cool breeze caressed my skin.

I can't lie. Victor had me feeling *too* good. Shoot, he almost had me thinking I was a perfect size six. He made me feel like I was Janet Jackson—"That's The Way Love Goes"—fine. As a matter of fact, if anyone had tried to tell me I wasn't fine, I would've looked at them like they'd lost their mind.

I smiled as I took in my surroundings. From the sky to the ocean to the people, Brazil was beautiful. And right about then, so was I.

***

Victor arrived at my door ten minutes early, and after we tried out the bed again, we headed to the lobby where I waited for Victor to pull his car around. After about five minutes, Victor returned to the lobby and grabbed my hand. I smiled as he wrapped his arm around my thick waist and guided me out of the hotel. I could feel envious eyes all around us as they burned holes into my flesh. Yeah, I was with what had to be the finest man in Rio, and I was proud of it.

When Victor led me out to the curb and opened the passenger door of a canary yellow Corvette Stingray, three things ran through my mind: Was this his car? How on Earth was he able to afford it? And, would I be able to fit in it? Well, the third question was answered pretty quickly. I slid into the car with no trouble, and as Victor settled into the driver's seat, I asked the first question.

"Is this your car?"

He smiled as he started the engine. "Yes. It was a gift."

I nodded. Someone *gave* him a Corvette? Okay, if there had been any doubt in my mind before, I was now sure that Victor was a gigolo. He had the car, the nice clothes, and he was just too good in bed. But he hadn't asked me for a dime. Maybe I was a charity case. I really didn't care. Being with Victor beat being alone and hurt.

"What is your family name, Alexandria?" he asked as he navigated the busy streets of Rio.

"Weaver. What's yours?"

"Castro."

"Victor Castro. That's a nice name."

"Thank you. So is yours."

"My friends call me Alex."

He shook his head. "Alexandria is too beautiful to be shortened. I will always call you Alexandria."

I silently wished "always" was longer than the five days I had left to spend in Rio. "Are you originally from Rio? Did you grow up here? Are you Portuguese?" I asked, finally getting more acquainted with a man I'd had sex with—oh, who was I kidding? I'd lost count of the number of times we'd had sex in the last two days.

"I am African, French, and Portuguese—mostly Portuguese, and I am from São Paulo. My cousin manages the hotel, and when she offered me a job, I moved here. I think she wants to fire me now." He ended his statement with a devilish grin.

I frowned. "Why? You are very good at what you do." *All of what you do.*

He glanced over at me. "I cause her much trouble. I do not try, but I always do."

I bet you do. "Victor, are you a gigolo?"

He laughed. "What?"

"Do… do women pay you for sex?"

He shrugged. "Sometimes."

I was speechless for a moment. I guess I was surprised at how easily he'd admitted it. I turned and looked out the window and noticed that instead of tall, shiny buildings, we were passing shanty houses. We were entering the favelas.

I turned and looked at Victor. "Why?" I asked.

"Why do women pay me for sex? Because I am good at it," he said matter-of-factly

I know that's right, I thought. "No, why do you *let* women pay you for sex?"

"Because I like women, I like sex, and I like money," he said as if he was ticking off the reasons he liked a certain TV show, or something as mundane as that.

"How many women have you been with?"

"Ah... *many.*"

"Okay... so why haven't you asked me for money?"

He glanced over at me. "Because I find pleasure in you. You're here because you need something, and I want to give it to you."

"What do you mean?"

"You were hurt. Someone you loved treated you badly. I'll treat you well, and when you return to United States, you'll have nothing but good thoughts of Rio."

I smiled. "And of Victor."

He returned my smile. "Yes."

He pulled to a stop in front of what looked like an open-air market, opened the door for me, and took my hand. After I climbed out of the car, he pulled me into his arms, softly kissed my neck, and dragged his lips to my mouth. My whole body smiled.

"Ah, there is my smile again. You are so beautiful when you

smile."

I couldn't stop smiling. "Where are we?" I asked.

"This is a Carnival celebration. We're going to dance and drink, and later, we'll make love all night."

Well, at least he was straight forward—no beating around the bush. And we did just what he said. We ate and drank, and at first, we watched as the favela's samba school danced to the pulsating, Afro-Brazilian rhythms. I tapped my feet to the music as Victor stood behind me, his hands on my hips. After a few songs, he whirled me around and began to dance with me. "Do you feel the music?" he whispered in my ear.

I nodded as he pulled me closer to him. The dance we shared felt much more intimate than any time we'd spent together in bed. As the music throbbed, it seemed to become a part of us, a part of the internal rhythms of our hearts, of our souls. With that dance, I saw through the handsome face and the gorgeous body to the essence of who Victor was as a man. And I saw to the core of who I was as a woman.

Hours later, we returned to the hotel, exhausted, sweaty, and stimulated at the same time. He spent the night with me, and I wished the night would never end.

7

"Don't Take It Personal"

Victor Castro was a very well-connected man. I received some decent Sambadrome tickets with my vacation package, but Victor somehow managed to get us seats near the parade judges. So we had a near perfect view of the samba schools as they paraded and performed.

I must've taken a million pictures of the elaborate costumes and floats, but one really needed a video camera to capture the full glory of Rio's Carnival Parade. I was in awe of the precision of their performances—the speed of their feet and the quick movements of their hips. Victor told me that the samba schools devoted most of their time throughout the year to preparing for Carnival, and I believed him.

The Sambadrome was full of people, *thousands* of people. And the excitement of the celebration was electrifying and infectious. We never took our seats, but stood there late into the night, cheering and singing along with the music—or at least I tried to. Victor held me closely and danced with me, his eyes bright with excitement. He loved Rio and he loved Carnival, and so did I.

***

I had two days left in Rio. Two more days and then back to reality. Two more days and no more Ipanema Beach at a luxury hotel. Two more days and no more Carnival. Two more days and no more Victor Castro. I was definitely going to miss him.

I'd spent a lot of time with Victor—in and out of bed—and we'd actually gotten to know each other. I learned that he loved Brazilian jazz, cold beer, and of course, sex. He was thirty-three, had never been married, no kids. He said he didn't have a girlfriend, but I found that hard to believe. Either the women in Brazil were blind and crazy, he was lying, or he was actually gay. And if he was gay, he was very good at acting straight. Anyway, he denied being gay when I asked, so that was not the situation. The only explanation I could come up with for his singleness was his job. Maybe he saw a relationship as an occupational hazard. Whatever was the case, I liked Victor, and I really felt we'd made a connection, a bond.

We were sitting on my balcony early in the morning, having spent another night together. We were tangled in each other's arms with our lips locked in a passionate kiss. That was the one thing I'd miss most about Victor—his kisses. When he kissed me, it was as if he was trying to explore my soul, trying to get to the core of who I was down to the most intimate detail and the deepest secret. He was just as much an expert at kissing as he was at everything else, maybe even more so. As far as I was concerned, they needed to change the name from French kissing to *Brazilian* kissing, because *this* Brazilian had mastered the technique. "Two days left," I whispered breathily once our kiss had ended.

"You do not want to leave?" he asked.

"Of course not. This is paradise. I've enjoyed being here so much. I'm not looking forward to going back and having to face what's left of my life."

"I'm sorry."

I shook my head. "It's my own fault. I just wanted to get married and have a family so badly that I pushed him before he was ready. Now, I'll probably never have a family."

"You want children?"

"More than anything. But I want to be married and in love, also. That's just the way I was raised. My mother drilled it into me from the time I was a little girl—marriage, then children."

"You can adopt a baby, yeah?"

"I could, but I'd rather carry a child."

We were both quiet for a few minutes before Victor spoke again. "Maybe I can help you."

I smiled and kissed his cheek. "Wouldn't it be nice if you could? No, I just have to face the facts and go on living my life."

"No, listen to me. I can help you. I'll marry you and give you children, as many as you like."

"What? You want to marry me? You don't even know me, Victor. And I don't know you. And we are not in love."

"You want children, yeah?"

"Yes, but I can't ask you to do something like this."

"You could pay me," he said matter-of-factly.

I stood from my seat on the lounger and frowned. "So this is what this is all about, what *everything* has been about? That's why you've been spending time with me for free? So you can scam me later?"

"Scam?"

"Yes, you think I'm some kind of desperate, rich fool or something? Well, I'm not. And you can leave."

He stood to face me. "I was not trying to upset you, Alexandria. And I told you, I find pleasure in you, and I never mix business with pleasure. What I am proposing is a business arrangement. I marry you, I give you children, you pay me, and I leave."

I folded my arms over my chest. "I want a *real* marriage and a *real* family, not some business deal. I want *love*, Victor."

"Time is leaving you, yes?"

My frown deepened. "What?"

"You're not getting any younger, Alexandria."

"You need the money that bad? You gotta insult me?"

He rested his hands on my arms. "I like you, and I want to help you."

"For a price."

"I have needs."

I sighed. "Get out."

He stared at me and then softly kissed my cheek. "Okay, I will go. You have my card. If you change your mind, call me."

"Don't count on it," I scoffed. "You're not *that* good. I ain't about to pay for it!" Well, actually he *was* that good. Shoot, he was so good, I finally understood what people meant when they referred to looking for someone in the daytime with a flashlight. But there was no way I was going to take him up on his insanely insulting offer. *No way!*

He flashed me a smile as he slid out the door.

I was mad as hell, but I shouldn't have been. After all, he was a gigolo, had readily admitted it. And besides, from the moment he saw me, I probably had "Sucker!" stamped on my forehead. Crying all over him didn't help. Neither did jumping in bed with him without question or concern. Boy, was I an easy mark.

***

As I snaked my way through the crowded Houston airport, my legs felt as heavy as lead. I was tired. Not tired from my trip, but tired from the thoughts that invaded my mind the last hours of my time in Rio. Thoughts of the empty home I would walk into in just minutes. Thoughts of Quincy's betrayal. The pain was still there—not paralyzing or unbearable as before, but it was still there like a dull, annoying ache that just wouldn't go away. When I was with Victor, I almost thought it was gone for good, but as I sat alone in my room, packing for the trip back home, I felt the feelings resurface. I felt the sting again.

I fought tears all the way through the airport to my car. Then I sat behind the wheel and stared at the people as they climbed in and out of their cars. I listened as they dragged their bags across the concrete floor of the parking deck. I didn't want to go home and be alone.

After thirty minutes of sitting and staring, I sighed and started my car. And before I knew it, I was pulling into my driveway. I parked my car, relieved that the driveway was empty. I had half-expected my mom or Gwin to have planned a welcome home bash, and Lord knows I wasn't in the mood for that. The only thing I wanted to do was climb into my bed and sleep the remainder of my time on this earth away.

I pulled my luggage from the trunk and made my way to the door.

As I walked inside, I sighed woefully, dropped my bags, and turned to lock the door. I nearly jumped out of my skin when I heard several voices yell, "Surprise!"

Well, hell, I thought.

I shook my head, plastered on a terribly unconvincing smile, and turned around. I was greeted by the smiling faces of my mother, Gwin, a few of my cousins, Farrah's two kids, and some ladies from my church.

"Oh, wow," I said. "Y'all shouldn't have gone through all this trouble for me. But, thank you."

Gwin grabbed me and pulled me into a tight hug. "Your mama made me help her. I knew you wouldn't like it," she whispered.

"It's all right," I whispered back. But it wasn't.

She released me, and then it was my mother's turn to pull me into a hug. "I'm so glad you made it home safely. You done been in the sun too much, though. Girl, you darkened up!" she said. My mom had a thing about skin color.

"Um, yeah, Rio is all about sun and fun," I replied in a marginally enthusiastic tone.

"I bet," a voice at the back of the room said. My mouth dropped open.

Surely goodness and mercy that is not who I think it is.

But it was, because the next face to emerge from the crowd was my sister, Farrah's. I looked at Gwin who shook her head and mouthed, *I tried to tell her.* Then she nodded towards Mama.

"Mama, can I speak to you in the kitchen, please?" I said through my teeth.

Mama nodded and with a look on her face that read "busted," she followed me from the foyer into the kitchen. "What is it, baby?" she asked innocently.

"Excuse my language, and know that I mean no disrespect, but what the hell is Farrah doing in my house?"

"She's your sister, and she feels bad about what she did."

I could not believe my mother! "Mama, no she doesn't! Farrah never feels bad about anything she does. She's a sociopath, if you ask me. She doesn't care about me, and I doubt she cares about Quincy. She doesn't even care about her own kids!"

"Hold your voice down, and watch your language. You have guests out there!"

"I didn't invite them! You had no business letting Farrah into my house. I gave you that key for emergencies, and you used it for evil!"

"Now, Alex, you need to calm down, Farrah is your family. You can't stay mad at her forever; you need to forgive her, and you two need to move past this."

"That trick hasn't even apologized, and you want me to forgive her? Are you serious?!"

"You ain't got to call me no trick, Alex," Farrah said. She stood just inside the kitchen doorway.

"Get out of my house," was my response.

"See, Mama. I told you she would act like this. She acts like I did it on purpose or something," Farrah said.

With widened eyes, a furrowed brow, and an impending

headache, I said, "What are you talking about? What happened, Farrah? Did you accidentally stumble into my man's house and by happenstance take your clothes off and then fall on his penis?"

She shrugged. "Something like that."

My whole body shook with rage, and before I knew it, I was screaming, "Get out! Get out! GET OUT OF MY HOUSE, FARRAH!!"

"Alex—" Mama began.

"No! I want everybody out! This is *my* house. *I* pay the note. I want everybody out of here, *now!*"

Mama shrunk away from me and slid out of the kitchen right behind Farrah, who looked rather frightened. The next thing I heard was the bustling of the crowd as they left my home.

I sat down at my kitchen table and gripped my head in my hands as I tried to calm myself. I closed my eyes and tried not to think about killing Farrah, but the images of me hurting her just would not leave.

"Alex," a small voice said.

I looked up and saw Gwin standing before me, concern in her eyes. "I'm sorry," she added.

I closed my eyes again. "It's not your fault."

"I'm gonna clean up and then leave. Do you need anything before I go?"

I looked up at her and the tears I'd been fighting back finally began to fall. I shook my head. "Can you stay for a little while? I don't want to be alone right now."

She nodded. "Okay." She sat down next to me and wrapped her arm around my shoulder as I cried. We sat there for hours before Gwin finally left, and I went to bed.

8

"Something In The Past"

I was in no mental state to be writing, and I knew it. But writing was my passion and my refuge and when all else failed, only it could lift my mood. But somehow, the depression I'd slid back into as soon as my plane hit US soil had superseded the healing effects of writing. Sitting on my computer screen was not the elegant string of words I was known for, but a string of obscenities. Nothing but angry words lined the page.

I sighed, closed my eyes, and prayed for a brief moment. Then I clicked on the iTunes icon and began to scroll through my music, hoping that a soothing tune would inspire me. Why in the world did I own so many stupid love songs? I scrolled and scrolled until my only option for music was a Lil' Wayne album that Quincy had downloaded to my computer, and I couldn't even stand to listen to that, because it reminded me of him.

I stared at the songs listed on the computer: "What You Won't Do For Love," "Can't Hide Love," "Love And Happiness," "Sweet Love," "When We Get Married," and the one that really sent me over the edge: "All True Man." That did it. Next thing I knew, I was deleting my entire iTunes library. Then I deleted the page of obscenities.

Then I unplugged the laptop and threw it across the room. Somehow it landed on the couch, and just as I was walking over to it with intentions of thrusting it against the wall, my doorbell rang. At first I stood there as if I didn't know what to do. Then I slowly made my way to the door, smoothing my hand over the raggedy braids on my head. I peered through the peep hole and felt my blood instantly begin to boil. I snatched the door open and shrieked, "What the hell do you want?!"

A startled Quincy fell to his knees as if on cue. "I-I-I came to beg for your forgiveness," he stuttered.

I slammed the door in his face and leaned against it.

"Please, Alex! Please, just let me in. Let me apologize to you, and then I'll leave, I promise," he begged through the door.

I shut my eyes tightly and gritted my teeth. "Get off of my property, Quincy!"

"Alex, I'm out here on my hands and knees. Your neighbors are staring at me. I love you, Alex. I'm begging you. Please, baby. *Please*, just let me apologize."

"You can apologize through the door."

"No, I can't. I need to look you in the eye so you can see I'm for real. Please, baby. I can't sleep. I can't eat. *Please*."

I lightly rested my head against the door and groaned. I took a few breaths and then opened it. Quincy was still on his knees. "Get up," I said, then turned and walked into my living room. I set the laptop on the coffee table and sat on the sofa. "You've got five minutes."

He nodded and sat across from me on the love seat. "Okay."

We sat in silence for a minute.

"Talk!" I shouted.

"O… okay. Look, baby. There's really no excuse for what I did. Farrah'd been trying to get with me for a long time, but I always made it clear that I wasn't interested. I was feeling a lot of pressure—about the wedding and everything—and when she showed up that morning, I guess I was just feeling a little vulnerable."

I shook my head. "You shouldn't have agreed to marry me if you weren't ready."

"I didn't think I had a choice. I didn't want to lose you, because no matter what you may think of me, I really do love you. I went along with the wedding, because I needed you. I still need you… and I miss you."

I leaned forward. "Maybe you do love me, Q. A part of me believes that you really do. But no matter how pressured you felt, you should not have relieved that pressure with my sister's vagina. There is *no* excuse for that."

"I know that. I'm just asking you to give me another chance. I just want you to forgive me."

I sighed. "I can't. And even if I could forgive you, I couldn't forget. "

He fell to his knees and crawled over to me. "Will you at least try? Give me a week. Let me show you that I love you. I miss you, baby. And I am *so sorry*."

I looked down at him. "Why Farrah? Why my sister? Of all the people in the world, why her?"

He dropped his eyes. "I don't know."

Despite my best efforts not to, I began to cry. I was so tired of crying. "She has everything. She has children. She found a man who was willing to marry her—no pressure. And then she took from me the only man I ever loved. Why? *Why*?" I hung my head and sobbed.

He reached up and embraced me. "I'm sorry, baby. I'm so sorry. She didn't take me. I'm yours." He rocked me back and forth.

He soothed me for several minutes—until I ran out of tears to cry. Then he released me and kissed me softly. "If you just give me a chance, *one chance*, I'll make it up to you. Will you let me? Please, Alex?"

I stared at him. I guess I was just tired. Tired of hurting and tired of being angry. "Yes," I said softly.

Quincy sat down on the sofa beside me and kissed me tenderly. Then he stood and led me to my bedroom.

***

Quincy spent the next two weeks trying to prove his love to me. He spent just about every moment he wasn't at work with me. And when he was at work, he called me every hour. He had flowers sent to my house every day. He cooked for me, gave me massages, and bathed me. He gave me the passcode to his cell phone, and I didn't even ask for it. Now *that* blew my mind! And if his phone rang while we were together, he asked me to answer it. That never happened when we were together before.

All in all, those two weeks were good, and I felt some of the sadness lift. I have to admit that it felt good to be back with Quincy. After all, I did love him and had spent a lot of years building a relationship with him. If nothing else, I was comfortable with him. So he wasn't as skilled as Victor. That was okay, because what Victor had to offer was dangerous. Victor was the type of man a woman could lose herself for. He was downright addictive. And that was the last thing I needed.

On this particular Friday night, we were together at my house since I still couldn't bring myself to go over to the scene of the crime—his place. We were watching a DVD in my living room, eating popcorn, and just enjoying each other's company. It was nice and relaxing and familiar, and I loved it. Halfway through the movie, he excused himself to the bathroom and seconds later, his phone rang. The screen read: *unavailable*.

"Q, your phone!" I yelled from my seat on the sofa.

"Answer it, baby!" he yelled back.

I picked up the phone, accepted the call, and said, "Hello?"

Silence on the other end.

"Hello?"

"Is Q there?" said a female voice. A voice that sounded familiar to me—*too* familiar.

I took a deep breath, steadied my hands, counted to three, and said, "Farrah?"

"Yeah, who is this?"

I answered with, "Why are you calling Quincy?"

"Alex?"

"I repeat: why are you calling Quincy?"

"Y'all back together?" Her shock registered loud and clear in her voice.

I held the phone and tried to calm myself.

"Oh, so you can forgive him, but you can't forgive your own sister? That's real messed up."

"I don't know why I'm still on this phone with you knowing you are only calling to start some mess. Bye, Farrah." I ended the call and laid the phone down and stared at it, waiting for it to ring again. I was still staring at it when Quincy returned to the room.

He plopped down on the sofa and said, "Who was it?"

I shifted my gaze from the phone to his face. "Farrah."

He jumped up from the sofa and grabbed the phone. "What?! What did she want?!"

I looked up at him. "Why don't *you* tell *me*?"

"I don't know! I haven't talked to her since we…"

I stared at him in silence.

"Okay, okay, let me call her and we'll straighten this out right now. What's her number?"

I rolled my eyes. "Like you don't know."

"Come on, baby. Just give me the number."

I rattled off Farrah's number and watched as he dialed it and activated the speakerphone. It rang three times before Farrah answered. "Hello?"

"Farrah? It's Quincy. Why did you call me? I'm trying to work things out with Alex, and I don't need you contacting me."

"Yeah, well that's cute and everything, but I'm afraid we gon' be having a lot of contact from now on."

Quincy shook his head. "No, we're not. We're done. It was a one-time mistake that I am trying to move past. There's nothing between us."

"Q, I'm pregnant," she said. I felt my breath catch in my throat.

Quincy frowned. "What does that have to do with me?"

"It's yours."

9

"Another Way"

When I came to myself, my house was full of policemen, my mother was sitting on the sofa crying, and Gwin was yelling at Quincy, who had a bloody nose and a black eye. I looked around the room at the pillows strewn all over the place, the broken glass of the end table, my flat-screen television which was lying face-down on the floor, the popcorn that littered the floor like yellow snowflakes, and it all came rushing back to me.

After Farrah's revelation, I snapped. I mean I *literally* snapped and lost total and complete control of myself. I started swinging on Quincy—wildly punching and kicking him with all of my might. He never fought back. He just stood there and tried to block my blows while screaming that Farrah was lying. I remember him running from the room, and I guess that's when he called the police and Mama and Gwin.

I was sitting on the loveseat, my eyes taking in the scene. I was embarrassed and angry and sad all at the same time. And even though I had to agree with Quincy that Farrah was probably lying (I wouldn't have put it past her to lie just to get money from him for some fake abortion), the fact that it was even a possibility tore right through my heart. What if it was true? For so long I had wanted nothing more than to become Quincy's wife and have his child. The idea of Farrah being pregnant by him was just too much.

I looked at one of the officers through vacant eyes and asked, "Am I under arrest?"

The officer shook his head. "No, ma'am. Mr. Wright has declined to press charges. But I would advise you to get some help. You seem to have some anger issues."

I didn't reply, because anything that came out of my mouth would probably have made him change his mind about arresting me.

A few minutes later, the policemen left.

"Mama, you should go on home. I'm fine now," I said.

"You sure? I could stay the night."

"I'm positive. Quincy's going to leave, too."

Mama nodded, grabbed her purse, and left the room. Gwin walked her to the door.

Quincy stood next to the toppled-over TV and stared at me.

"You heard me. *Leave*," I demanded.

"No. You know Farrah's lying, Alex. You *know* that!"

"It doesn't matter anymore. I can't be with you. Just leave. I'm too tired to do this tonight."

He opened his mouth to speak and then seemed to change his mind. He grabbed his phone and car keys. "Okay. I love you, Alex. I'll call you tomorrow."

I didn't respond.

He left as Gwin returned to the living room. "Quincy told me what Farrah said. You don't believe her, do you?"

"No, but I don't believe him, either. And I can't get over the fact that it's even a possibility." I looked up at her. "I tried, Gwin. I really tried to work things out with him, because I truly love him. But..."

She sat down beside me and rested her hand over mine. "It's okay. I understand."

"This makes me wish I'd taken Victor up on his offer," I muttered.

"Victor? *Rio* Victor? What offer?"

I'd filled her in on my time with Victor and his... *skills*, but I hadn't told her about his little offer. I looked over at her and shook my head. "Nothing. I'm just talking out of my head right now."

"Okay. Look, I gotta head back home. You sure you're okay? You could come with me and sleep in the spare bedroom."

"No, I'm fine. I'ma go to bed and try to get some rest."

She hugged me. "Okay. Love you, girl."

"Love you, too."

***

I spent the next week trying to get some rest, I guess, because in those seven days, I only left the bed to use the toilet or answer the door. And the only reason I answered the door was because I ordered deliveries of food every day. Other than that, I burrowed deep beneath the covers and stared into the darkness. I didn't cry. Evidently I was past the crying phase. I didn't yell or scream, or have the desire to destroy things, either. I had already been through the denial stage when I attempted to reconcile with Quincy. Now, I had moved on to acceptance. I accepted that it was over between me and Quincy. I accepted that I'd wasted eight good, viable-egg years of my life. I accepted that my little sister would stop at nothing to make me miserable. I accepted that I would probably never fall in love again or get married or worst of all, have children. I accepted that I'd never have a family—no baseball games or dance recitals were in my future. I accepted that I was powerless to change my inevitable future. I accepted that no one could help me. I was alone, and I'd always be alone.

"Victor can help you," a small voice inside of my head said.

I laughed out loud. "No way. I am not desperate enough to *pay* a man to give me children," I said to the empty room.

"Time's running out. It took eight years to get Quincy to marry you. Do you have eight more years to waste?"

"But I want to be in love when I get married and have children."

"You love Victor's sex, don't you? That's got to count for something."

"Yeah, I definitely love his sex. I love it a lot—*a whole lot*."

I sat up in the bed and shook my head at my own thoughts and words. *I'm going crazy. I am losing my mind. I am having a conversation with myself!*

"What's so crazy about taking control of your future?"

Okay, so that last thought actually made a lot of sense. It made so much sense that the next thing I knew, I was picking up my telephone, dialing Quincy's number. He answered before the first ring ended. "Hello? Alex?"

"Do you know a good international law attorney?" I said—no greeting. I didn't have time for greetings.

"Well, yeah. You working on a new distribution deal or

something?"

"Something like that."

"Well, Erica Dobson is the best international law attorney I know. Want me to call her for you?"

"Yes. I need to speak with her as soon as possible."

"Sure thing. Um, Alex, how've you been?"

I hesitated. "Fine."

"Good."

"Can you call her now?"

"Yeah, sure."

"Thank you."

"No problem."

I hung up and sat anxiously by the phone for the next thirty minutes. By the time I received the call from Attorney Erica Dobson, I had just about talked some sense into myself.

After answering with an anxious, "hello," I heard her voice on the other end.

"Ms. Weaver? This is Erica Dobson."

"Yes, thanks for calling. I'm sure Quincy told you about our connection."

"Well... yes."

"Okay, I need to be sure that you will keep my business strictly confidential."

"Of course. Under attorney-client privilege, I cannot divulge anything we discuss."

"Good. I want to retain your services. I'm planning to broker a deal with a gentleman in Rio de Janeiro, and I want the details kept confidential."

"That is no problem at all. What type of deal is it?"

"I need you to draft a pre-nuptial agreement."

"A... a pre-nup?"

"Yes. And I need to know how I would go about getting married in Brazil—what steps I need to take, how to get a marriage license, etcetera."

"Um... are you sure about this? I was under the assumption that you and Mr. Wright—"

"Well, you assumed wrong, I'm marrying a gentleman named Victor Castro—a citizen of Brazil. I need to know how to legally go about doing that. And I also need a clear and concise pre-nup. And I need all of that without fear of Quincy Wright or anyone else finding out. Can you do that?"

"Um... well, yes. If that's what you want."

"Great. I'll call Victor and get his lawyer's information so we can get the ball rolling. Thank you, Ms. Dobson."

"You're welcome," she said with a question in her voice.

I hung up, opened the drawer to the nightstand, dug beneath the papers, and found Victor's card hidden at the bottom. I flipped it over and dialed his number.

A female answered with a phrase in Portuguese that I didn't understand. "I'd like to speak with Victor Castro," I said, hoping she'd at least understand his name.

There was silence, then muffled voices, one of which I recognized as Victor's. Then I heard the phone click. I took the phone from my ear and looked at it. *Did they hang up on me?* I started to call back then decided that this was a sign. This was a crazy idea, and I knew it. The call had disconnected because it was wrong to arrange a marriage like a business deal, no matter the motive.

I laid my cell phone down on the nightstand and sighed. I decided to call Erica Dobson back in the morning and tell her to forget the whole thing. I'd just pay her whatever I owed her and move on with my poor, pitiful mess of a life—childless and husbandless.

I stood to my feet and had turned to leave the room when my phone began to buzz and vibrate against the nightstand. I stood there and stared at the number that flashed across the screen—*Victor's number*. I froze and stared at it until the words "missed call" appeared on the screen. Then I took a deep breath and sat back down on the side of the bed. I closed my eyes and jumped when the phone began to buzz again.

This time, I reached for it and for some reason, I answered it. "Hello?" I said hesitantly.

"This is Victor," said his familiar voice. "I believe we were disconnected?"

"Um… yes. Victor, it's Alex…Alexandria, from Texas. Do you remember me?"

"Alexandria! I've been awaiting your call."

"You have?"

"Yes. It is good to hear from you."

I smiled. I'd missed his heavily accented English. "Um, Victor.

Can you talk? Was I interrupting anything?"

"No. You want to talk business or pleasure?"

I smiled a little more. I'd missed Victor, all right—him and his considerable attributes. If I was to have a fake marriage with anyone, he was an excellent choice. "Both?"

"Okay."

"Do you have a lawyer?"

"Yes, I have a cousin who is a lawyer."

"Okay, before we hang up, I'll need for you to give me his or her contact information. I've decided to take you up on your offer, and we need to work out the details."

There was a moment of silence, and then Victor spoke again. "Are you sure you want to do this?"

I began to feel a little stupid. What if he'd changed his mind? "Uh… well, yes, if the offer still stands."

"Yes, it stands. But you know this will not be a marriage of love, yes? I know love is important to you. So again, I ask: are you sure you want to do this?"

I took a deep breath, and against my better judgment, said, "Yes, I'm sure."

"Good. Let's work out the details."

10

"Say Yeah"

It took two weeks for me and Victor to agree on the terms of our marriage. In exchange for marrying me and fathering at least two children, he would be paid a nice fee via a divorce settlement. I would take care of him financially during the marriage, of course. He was free to divorce me at any time after child number two's birth. If he decided to stay on and a third child was born, he'd receive a bonus. I was to assist him in gaining his citizenship so that he could visit the children freely after our divorce. I would retain full physical custody, of course. We would live in my home in Houston during the marriage, and he would not be allowed to take the children to Brazil without my knowledge and consent during or after the marriage. I also agreed that the firstborn male child would be named after Victor. He agreed that our firstborn female child would be named after my mother, Ruby.

The contract stipulated that no one was to know that this marriage was anything but legitimate. Victor was to live with me, accompany me to public events, and for all intents and purposes, behave like a loving husband. The contract was binding, but would be made void if he was found to have an STD or was infertile.

After all of the tests results were back—mine and his—it took another month and a half to get the Brazilian marriage license and set the date for the small wedding at Victor's uncle's church in São Paulo. This was the most complicated and in-depth project I'd ever worked on in my life, but if nothing else, it kept my mind off of Quincy, who continued to call nearly every day. And it kept me from following through on my thoughts of murdering my sister.

Other than telling them I was planning a return, mini-vacation trip to Brazil, Gwin and my mother had no idea about my plans. Neither did anyone else. I kept it under wraps, because I knew they'd try to talk me out of it. I knew they'd tell me I was making a mistake, and maybe I was. Mama would suggest that I speak with our pastor. I knew that was a good idea, but I felt that I was out of options. If I wanted a family, I needed to make a move and I needed to do it quickly. In my mind, hiring Victor was better than visiting some sperm bank. At least my children would be born into a marriage, and they would know who their father was. That had to count for something.

Now, I stood in my living room, my luggage piled up by the front door. I felt apprehensive about what I was about to do. Doubts screamed in my head so loudly that I barely heard the doorbell when it rang the first time. It rang again, and I pulled my purse strap over my shoulder and grabbed my luggage as I opened the door. On the other side stood my sister.

"What?" I grunted.

"Well, dang. Hello to you, too."

"Farrah, I haven't heard from you since you called my fiancé's phone with the wonderful news that you were pregnant by him. What did you expect?"

She shrugged. "Oh, that? False alarm."

I released a frustrated sigh. "You know what? You are going to play with the wrong person one day, and you are going to get hurt really bad, Farrah."

She rolled her eyes. "Yeah, well, I'll cross that bridge when I get to it."

"What do you want? I was just leaving for the airport, and I don't have time for you right now, so let me go ahead and say no, I don't forgive you for sleeping with Quincy. No, I'm not giving you any money. No, you can't borrow my car, and no, I can't keep your kids for you. That about cover it?"

"I really can't stand you," she hissed.

I shrugged. "Yeah, well, what's new? I tell you what. Whatever you need, why don't you go get it from Quincy?"

She dropped her eyes. "He won't answer the phone when I call."

"Sounds like a personal problem to me. Look, I gotta go. You can leave now."

She glared at me, then turned and stalked off muttering something under her breath. I shook my head as I set the alarm, then closed the door and loaded the luggage into my car. In no time, I was headed to the airport, on my way to take a step that I hoped would change my life forever.

***

Brazil was just as I left it—warm, inviting, and breathtakingly beautiful. Victor met me at the airport, and he was just as fine and handsome as I'd left *him*. He smiled and held my hand as he helped me with my luggage and steered me through the busy airport in São Paulo. We spent the night in a very nice hotel there in the city, getting reacquainted. I guess the whole not-seeing-the-bride-before-the-wedding thing didn't apply to us since this wasn't a real marriage.

The next morning, I dressed in a modest, mint green skirt and gold blouse and rode with Victor to a little church—the church where we were to be married with his uncle presiding. The church was filled to capacity with members of Victor's huge immediate and extended family. His mother, a wide and beautiful, caramel-skinned woman, sat proudly on the front pew, beaming at her youngest son. His brothers and sister flanked her wearing white smiles, all of them looking like gorgeous, bronze, curly-haired models for Brazilian travel posters.

Seeing the many happy faces of his family made me feel a little sad. For a moment, I wished my family was there, but then I remembered that they never would've approved of what I was doing. Instead of sitting on a pew with a proud smile, my mother would've been right up there at the altar with me, tugging on my arm while telling me that I was making a mistake. No, I'd made the right decision. And besides, Victor's mother seemed to understand when I told her my family was unable to travel to Brazil and that we would have another ceremony back home.

Thirty minutes after walking down the aisle of the small church, I was Mrs. Victor Castro. Victor's mother kissed me and hugged me tightly as did every single, solitary member of his family who was in attendance. One would've thought I'd always been a member of the family. And if they weren't hugging and kissing me, they were hovering near, smiling proudly. I have to admit, it felt good to be welcomed so warmly by them. It almost made me wish our union was not the result of a signed contract. I kind of wished I was actually becoming a permanent member of the family.

After the wedding, there was a celebration at Victor's mother's neat, split-level home which was located in the same neighborhood as the church. There was music and food galore—the kind of spread that could send a woman like me into hysterics. I couldn't pronounce the names of most of what I ate, but one didn't need to be able to speak Portuguese to know that everything was delicious. There was dancing and an almost constant outpouring of congratulations. There were wine and gifts and, though it wasn't some elegant affair at a luxury hotel, it was a wonderful event, a true celebration, and I enjoyed every second of it.

As the party began to wind down, Victor's mother pulled me to the side for a little chat.

She hugged me tightly and kissed both of my cheeks. Then she held my hands and gave me a warm smile. "I just want to thank you for this day. It is truly a day I never thought would come."

I squeezed her hands and returned her smile. "No, I should thank *you*. You have made this day so beautiful for us. Thank you for arranging everything. I'm sorry I couldn't help more, but it's hard to plan things when you're so far away."

She shook her head. "No, it was my pleasure. For so long, I feared Victor would never settle down. I did not think he would ever get married or have a family. And then he met you, and there was something about you that made him see the light and want to change the way he was living. You have stolen his heart. Now that he has you, I have no more worries about him." She held my face in her soft, warm hands. "Thank you, Alexandria."

I smiled and wanted to cry. I felt so bad about lying to her, but that's the way Victor wanted it. It was the way I wanted it, too. No one needed to know about the truth of our arrangement. If we told people, there would always be a chance that our children would find out, and I definitely didn't want that. So I covered Mrs. Castro's hands with my own, and said, "You're welcome. Thank you for letting me take your son away to the states."

She pulled me into another hug. "You will come back and visit often?"

I nodded against her shoulder. "We will."

As if he'd timed it, Victor found us, pulled me away from his mother, and gently kissed me.

"Thank you," he whispered into my ear as he took me into his arms and held me tightly.

I frowned. "For what?" I whispered back.

"For helping me make my mother so proud. I'll never forget this day."

I closed my eyes as he began to lead me in a dance. "Neither will I. Thank *you*."

11

"Sumthin' Sumthin'"

We spent the next two days in Brazil, working diligently on our first child. When we finally boarded the plane to return to the United States, I felt a little conflicted. I missed my home, but being in Brazil with Victor and his family had felt so... *good*. In Brazil, we were like a real couple. I enjoyed every moment of Victor showing me the sights of São Paulo. I enjoyed the weather, the food, the atmosphere, and the love. At least it *felt* like love. Victor was in love with Brazil for sure, and so was I. But there were also tender little moments when we were together—moments when he would reach for my hand, or gently caress my cheek—that I also felt like he loved me, and I felt like I could love him. In those moments, the gaping hole that Quincy left behind felt a little smaller.

As I settled into my seat on the plane, I closed my eyes and smiled a little. I allowed myself to consider what the future could hold for me and Victor. We were good together. We liked each other's company, and although what we had started out as a business arrangement, maybe it could eventually evolve into something more, something deeper. I opened my eyes and looked over at him. He was reclined in his seat with his eyes closed. He was so handsome—the total package. I could get used to being his wife.

But then reality sunk in. This wasn't real. I was paying him to be my husband and to father my children. I was paying him to play a role—to live a lie. I was flying back home to live a lie. I was getting ready to perpetrate a lie to everyone I knew and loved. Was I making a mistake?

My head began to ache. Talk about buyer's remorse. Up until that point, I really thought I was doing the best thing for myself. I wanted a family, but I wanted to do things the right way—get married first, then have kids. But how was this right? Victor and I didn't love each other. No, this was wrong. I closed my eyes and shook my head. It was too late, wasn't it? The contracts had been signed, vows had been recited. How could I possibly turn back?

"Alexandria, are you all right?" Victor asked softly.

I opened my eyes and looked over at him. So handsome. So sexy. But not really mine. "No."

With raised eyebrows, he said, "Having second thoughts?"

"And third and fourth thoughts."

He reached for my hand and gripped it tightly. "Why?"

"Be... because this is not right. I... I should've prayed about this first. I think I was just acting off of my emotions. I mean, I was supposed to be in love before I got married. I *was* in love..."

He shrugged. "Maybe you were acting off of emotions. Maybe this was a mistake. But what's done is done. We have a deal, Alexandria. I do not break deals."

"Is the money that important to you?"

"Yes, among other things."

I looked him in the eye. "Victor, I don't think I can go through with this."

Victor released my hand and rested his head against the seat. "Yes, you can. You want children, yeah?"

"Yes, of course I do, but—"

"Then it is too late to change your mind."

I frowned. "How so?"

He turned his head and smiled at me. "Well, if I am anything like my brothers, you're already pregnant. So, it is too late."

I leaned back against my seat and gazed out the window, unsure of how to feel.

Victor reached for my hand again. "We can give it a couple of weeks, yeah? If you still feel the same, we can forget the contract."

I looked over at him. "Really?"

"Yes, really."

"What about the money?"

"I have money. I would like to have *more* money, but I will not suffer without it."

I sighed. "Okay."

***

We arrived at my house to no surprise guests or visitors, thank goodness. My home was just as I left it—neat and in order. Victor took his time and looked around and seemed impressed with my place. When he made it to my bedroom, he smiled.

"Very nice bed," he said as he leaned over and kissed my cheek. He slowly slid his hand down my back. I shivered.

He looked around the room, focusing on the dresser. "Which drawers are mine? Did you make room in the closet for me?"

I clasped my hands in front of me. "You... you want to sleep in here... with me?"

He placed his hands on my shoulders. "Where else will I sleep?"

I shrugged. "I don't know. I guess I thought you'd rather sleep in one of the guest bedrooms, since this isn't a real marriage."

He kissed me slowly on the lips. "It is as real as we make it. And remember, there's business and there's pleasure. Taking vows was business, making love to you is always a pleasure for me." He kissed my neck. "Hmm, as a matter of fact, I would like some pleasure right now. Wouldn't you?"

I smiled and nodded as he led me to my bed. Now, who could argue with that logic?

12

"Nobody's Business"

The first week of my marriage was spent in and out of bed. We ate a little, slept a little, loved a whole lot. I definitely wasn't complaining. Like I said, Victor was very good at what he did. Excellent, really. This part of the deal was definitely a perk I enjoyed.

There was really no time for regrets at that point, because if I had viable eggs and Victor had good swimmers, I was most likely pregnant, or at least I hoped so. As I lay in bed next to him, his arm across my waist, I thought to myself that if things stayed this way, I could see myself being married to him for a very long time.

My cell phone began to buzz on the night table. I knew it was either Gwin or my mother—both of whom I'd been avoiding since making it back home from Brazil. I knew if I didn't answer soon, one of them was bound to just show up at my front door, and I wasn't ready for that. So I slowly climbed out of bed, leaving Victor behind as I grabbed my phone and tipped out into the hall.

"Hello?" I said, answering Gwin's call.

"Where in the world have you been?!" she shrieked into the phone. "I've been worried to death! You were supposed to make it back home a week ago!"

"I did."

"Then why on Earth haven't you been answering my calls? Did something happen in Brazil? Are you okay?"

"I'm fine, Gwin. I just needed some time alone."

"You were alone in Brazil, Alex. You don't get to be alone here."

"Really? Who are you? My guardian?"

"No, I'm your best friend, and I need to know what's going on with you."

"Nothing. Nothing is going on."

"And why haven't you talked to Ms. Ruby since you've been back? She's worried sick!"

I sighed. "I'll call my mother as soon as we hang up."

"Something ain't right, Alex."

"What are you talking about?"

"You sound too calm and peaceful. Something must've happened."

"So something has to be wrong with me because I'm calm. Dang, have I been that much of a basket case lately?"

"Well, yeah, you have. Where are you?"

"At home—in bed."

Ding dong!

"That's me at the door. Let me in," she said.

"What?! You've been outside this whole time?"

"Yeah, now let me in."

As I turned around, Victor came out of the bedroom. "Is that the door?"

I nodded as I passed him and headed back into the bedroom for my robe. "Is that the TV? I thought I heard a man's voice," Gwin said.

"Look, I'm coming," I replied as I ended the call. I shrugged into my robe and said, "That's my friend, Gwin, at the door. Could you stay up here until I get rid of her?"

Victor shrugged. "Sure."

I left the bedroom, trotted down the stairs, and unlocked the door. I'd barely opened it when Gwin shoved past me and rushed into the house. I was sure if the chain hadn't been on the door she would've used her key. My eyes widened as I watched my mother walk in behind her.

"Mama?"

"Yes, *Mama*," my mother replied. "What in the world been wrong with you? You go across the world and come back and don't even bother to call and tell your own mother you made it okay?"

I rubbed my forehead, glanced at the staircase. "I texted you when I got back. I texted *both* of you. I said I would call you later."

"Um, Alex, it's way past later. What's going on with you? I mean, you look good, *really* good, but you're acting *really* strange," Gwin replied. She stepped closer to me, her eyes glued to my neck. "Is that a hickey?" she whispered.

My hand flew to my neck. "What? Look, y'all, nothing is wrong—"

"Alexandria? Is everything okay down there?" Oh dear Lord, it was Victor. He was standing on the stairs, *shirtless*.

Gwin's and my mother's heads snapped towards the stairs then back at me, questions in their eyes and on the tips of their tongues, but before either of them could say a word, Victor walked down the stairs and over to me. He slipped his arm around my waist and kissed my cheek. "Who do we have here?" he asked.

"*Daaaamn…*" Gwin said softly, eying Victor from head to toe.

"Who is this, Alex?" Mama asked with a slight frown on her face.

I sighed. There was no avoiding it anymore. "Mama, Gwin, this is Victor—my husband."

"What?!" Gwin yelled.

Mama just stood there speechless before collapsing to the floor.

13

"Family Affair"

Mama regained consciousness a few minutes later. I sat on the couch next to her, holding her hand while Gwin held a cool towel to her forehead. Victor sat across from us, confusion on his face.

Mama opened her eyes and smiled at me. "Oh, Alex, I had the craziest dream. I dreamt you had married some guy I'd never seen before. He had an accent. I think he was a foreigner or something."

I patted her hand. "Mama—"

She looked across the room at Victor. "Aw, hell. I wasn't dreaming." She closed her eyes and placed her hand on her forehead.

"Mama, let me explain."

"Please do," Gwin said.

I sighed. "I met Victor when I went to Brazil the other month. We really hit it off, and when I went back last week, we decided to get married."

Gwin's eyes widened. "Y'all must have done a little more than hit it off. Alex, what is wrong with you? I mean, do you even *know* him?!"

"Yes, I do."

Victor stood from his seat. "I think I'll let you ladies speak privately. Alexandria, I will be in the kitchen."

I nodded as he walked over and kissed me on the cheek. "It was nice to meet you ladies," he added before leaving the room.

"Okay, first I gotta say this: that man is some kind of fine! Good Lord!" Gwin said as she fanned herself with her hand.

I grinned. "I told you he was."

"He's good looking, all right, but Alexandria Jeanine Weaver, what were you thinking, marrying some foreign man you've only known for a few months and bringing him here to live with you? He could be a killer or something. Do he even speak good English?"

"Why does he have to be a killer? He's been nothing but kind to me since the day I met him. And you know he speaks English; you just heard him."

"Is this about Farrah and Quincy?" Gwin asked. "Because neither of them is worth you throwing your life away. You need to think about what you're doing here, Alex. I mean, how long do you really expect this to last?"

I shrugged as I looked her in the eye. "I expect it to last as long as it lasts."

"What the crap does that mean?"

"It means, Gwin, that I am an adult—nearly forty years old. I married him because I wanted to. Look, thank you for being concerned about me, but I'm fine. Victor is good to me."

Mama struggled to her feet. "I need to go home. The longer I sit here and think about what you've done, the more my blood pressure goes up."

"Mama, are you okay to drive?" I asked.

"I'm fine. Gwin, I'll see you later. Alex, this discussion is not over. I'ma go home and take a nerve pill, and I'll deal with you later. I'm nervous as a whore in church right now."

I shook my head as I stood and kissed her cheek. "There's nothing to deal with, Mama. And stop being nervous. Everything'll be fine."

"Yeah, well, we'll see about that."

I walked Mama to the door and then returned to the living room where Gwin was waiting for me.

"Now that your mom is gone, tell me the truth. What's going on with you?" she said.

I plopped down on the sofa. "I told you already."

"No, you didn't. When you told me about Victor before, you said you had a good time with him, but I don't recall hearing anything about you loving him or wanting to marry him."

I stared at her for a moment. There was no sense in lying to Gwin, because of everyone in my life, she knew me best. I took a deep breath and released it. "Okay, our marriage is more of an arrangement than an actual marriage."

"Arrangement?"

"A deal of sorts. We agreed to get married, and after we have two children, he is free to divorce me."

"Are you paying him, Alex?"

"If he fulfills his duties, yes, he will be compensated."

"Have you lost your mind?! Why would you do something like this?!"

"Because I've plenty of money, and I didn't feel like I had any other options. Look, Gwin, I'm not getting any younger. My relationship, a relationship it took *eight years* to build, is over. Don't you think I wanted to do this the right way? Don't you think this was a hard decision for me to make? I did what I felt I had to do. As my friend, *my best friend*, I'm asking you to accept my decision and support me. *And* to please keep this under wraps. "

"You know I'm not gonna tell anyone. And as your *best friend*, you could've told me what you were planning."

"No, I couldn't. You wouldn't have understood. "

Gwin sighed. "Did you pray before you made this decision, Alex?"

"No, because if I had, I wouldn't have done it."

"Do you hear how crazy that sounds?"

"I never prayed about my relationship with Quincy, either."

"And I guess that's supposed to make it seem less crazy to me?"

"Maybe it's crazy, maybe not. All I know is that Victor is kind to me, and he possesses everything I ever wanted in a husband."

"Really? What? Good looks and bedroom skills?"

"No, *amazingly* good looks, *exceptional* bedroom skills, *and* viable sperm."

She shook her head. "Lord help you."

"And when he speaks Portuguese? *Girrrrrl.*"

"Alex!"

"Look, I'm not like you. I didn't meet my soul mate in college and have two beautiful kids. I'm too old to be starting some new relationship. I did what I had to do."

She reached for my hand and squeezed it. "I just don't want anything to happen to you."

I smiled at her. "Nothing is going to happen to me. Victor's a perfect gentleman. I'm going to be fine, and I'm going to have some beautiful godchildren for you to spoil."

She nodded. "Well, one thing's for sure, you two will have some gorgeous kids. You said he was fine, but shoot!"

I laughed. "I know. That makes this whole arrangement even better."

Gwin stood from the sofa. "Look, I'm going to head on out. Sorry about showing up unannounced and busting up your honeymoon. I was just worried about you." She turned to leave and then added, "Hey, does Quincy know about this?"

I shook my head. "No."

She gave me a mischievous look. "He is gonna die when he finds out."

I shrugged. "Good."

"Okay, I see you still feel the same way about him. Anyway, I love you, Alex. Don't ever think you have to keep anything else from me. I'll always have your back, right or wrong, but as your friend it's my duty to try and talk some sense into you when I see you doing something reckless."

I hugged her. "I know that, but I promise you, I know what I'm doing, and everything will be fine."

"I sure hope so. Bye."

"Bye."

I shut the door behind her and just stood there for a moment, trying to make myself believe what I'd just told her. I wanted to believe that things would be okay, but honestly, I just didn't know.

"Everyone is gone?" Victor's voice brought me out of my thoughts.

I looked up at him. "Yes. Why didn't you stay upstairs like I asked?"

He shrugged. "I did not want to."

I sighed. "I wasn't ready to tell them about us."

He walked over to me and kissed me softly. "Well, now they know. So come back to bed."

"Victor—"

"What happened? Did the world end because they know?"

"Well... no."

"Then come back to bed."

"Victor, look, when it comes to my family and friends, I would appreciate it if you would respect my—"

He cut me off by leaning in and kissing me deeply. What else could I do but shut up and follow him upstairs. I mean, really?

***

Two weeks passed before I heard from my mother again, and all she had to say was that she was throwing a barbecue for Farrah's son's birthday, and she'd like for me to be there.

"Oh, and you can bring your *husband* if you want to, since it's a family affair," she said. Yep, she was still upset about the whole secret marriage thing.

I loved and respected my mother more than anyone else in the world. After she and my father divorced, she'd been a rock, raising Farrah and me alone until she married her second husband, Mr. Wesley, when I was fifteen and Farrah was nine. Mr. Wesley was a lot older than Mama, but he was nice enough, and Mama made sure he knew she was running the show when it came to me and my sister. He never spanked us or even said a harsh word to us, because Mama wasn't having it. Now Mr. Wesley was ailing, unable to get out of bed for more than a few minutes at a time, and Mama made sure he was well taken care of.

I rarely heard from my father after he left. We'd get the occasional birthday gift or Christmas card, and visits were nonexistent. My father remarried before the ink on his and my mother's divorce papers were even dry. And then he and his new wife moved out of state. Truthfully, it had been more than a decade since I'd spoken to him at all. He was pretty much a non-factor in my life. So it was hard on me to know that my mother was upset with me. It was even harder to lie to her. I just hated for her to be upset with me. Victor and I would have to work extra hard to appear as a blissfully happy, madly in love couple to ease her misgivings. When I told him this, he smiled and said, "I know my role, darling. I will play it fully. You just be sure to play yours."

I replied with, "I will."

I knew my family well enough to know that they never started anything on time, so we arrived at my mother's house about thirty minutes late, which would equal to on-time for her. To my surprise, her driveway was full of cars, and more cars lined the street from one block to the other. Quite a lot of people for a ten-year-old's birthday party.

I parked down the block, took a deep breath, and looked over at Victor. "You ready?"

He smiled and leaned over to kiss me. "Always."

We climbed out of the car and made the trek down the street to my mother's house—my childhood home. I closed my eyes and said a silent prayer before ringing the doorbell. My family was a trip, and Victor was a stranger to them. There was no telling how this day would play out.

The door swung open, and there stood Farrah. Okay, so it was her son's birthday and I knew she'd be there, but that didn't change the fact that I still despised her and hated to be in her presence. She gave me a familiar sneer before looking past me. Her eyes widened, and I swear she started drooling as she stood there staring at Victor. "Whoa! Mama said he looked good, but I just wasn't expecting *this*! You found him in Rio? He need a green card or something?"

I wanted to punch her lights out. Why did a man have to marry me solely for an upgrade in his immigration status? I just hated Farrah and her smart mouth.

Victor squeezed my shoulder with one hand and then extended the other one towards Farrah. "I'm Victor, and you are?"

Farrah grasped his hand, and I noticed that she held on to it when he tried to let go. "Oh, my God! That accent! It makes you want to just take your panties right off!" Farrah exclaimed.

"A warm breeze makes you want to take your panties off, you cheap tramp," I mumbled.

"What'd you say?" she asked as she glared at me.

Ignoring her question, I freed Victor's hand from her death grip, and said, "Victor, this is my tramp—uh, I mean my sister, Farrah.

Farrah, this is my *husband*, Victor."

I shoved Farrah out of the doorway and pulled Victor into the house. When we made it into the living room, the crowd of cousins and aunts and uncles instantly fell silent. Mr. Wesley was even sitting in his wheelchair in a corner with his mouth hung open. I swear the music that had been playing stopped. You could hear paint dry in that room.

Then the silence was broken with a couple of "damns" and at least one, "dang, he fine."

Victor gave me a confused look as he reached for my hand. Okay, maybe I should've told my family about the marriage beforehand, because the gawking and staring was very embarrassing.

"Everyone," I began. "This is my husband, Victor. Victor, this is my family."

"Very nice to meet all of you. I'm grateful to be part of such a beautiful family," Victor said graciously.

More gawking and stares until Aunt Nancy, my mother's sister, stepped forward and hugged Victor. "Good to meet you, Victor. I'm Aunt Nancy," she said. Then she turned to the rest of my family. "Don't just stand there looking crazy, let's give him a warm family welcome."

Mercifully, everyone seemed to snap out of their Victor-induced trance and began to step forward to shake his hand and hug him. The only snag after that was that I had to slap my cousin-in-law, Freda's, hand off of his butt. She was the widow of one of Aunt Nancy's sons, and she was an even bigger freak than my sister.

My cousin, Albert, stepped forward and in a way specific only to him said, "Dang, cuz, you dropped that big, light-bright, Shemar Moore-looking Negro for a Mexican, huh? You speak that Spanish or Spanglish or whatever it is?"

I wished I could've crawled under the sofa or a table or something and disappeared. I was so ashamed. "He's from Brazil, Al. They speak Portuguese there, but he knows English," I said.

"Ain't Mexico and Brazil like the same thing?"

"No, Al. They're on two different continents."

"Word? You learn something new every day. He got some good hair, too. He got any sisters?"

"Lord Jesus, save me," I muttered.

Thankfully, my other cousins, Brandon and Kringle (Yes, Kringle was his real first name) along with Albert, were in the middle of a domino game and decided to rope Victor into playing, figuring he'd be easy to beat. Well, they figured wrong. They were in the middle of a butt-whipping at his hand when my mother and Aunt Nancy approached me.

They flanked me on the sofa and each grasped one of my hands. "Well..." Aunt Nancy said.

I raised my eyebrows. "Well?"

"Well, he sure is good-looking."

I smiled. "Yes, ma'am."

Mama chimed in. "And he do seem nice."

I turned to face her. "He is. He's very nice. A complete gentleman."

"Mm-hmm. Well, then I wish the two of you the best," Aunt Nancy said.

"Thank you, Aunt Nancy. Mama?"

Mama squeezed my hand. "You know I just want you to be happy, sugar. Right?"

"I know, Mama. I *am* happy."

"Well, of course I wish you'd gotten married in our church, and I wish I could've been there. But, I still wish you two nothing but the best."

"Thank you, Mama. That means a lot to me."

We were interrupted by Victor, who leaned over, kissed my cheek, and said, "Can you excuse us, ladies? I would love to dance with my beautiful wife."

"Aye! You gon' do us like that, man?" said Albert before I could respond to Victor's request. "Cuz, why you ain't tell us that boy could play bones like that? Shoot, I ain't even know they could play bones in Mexico."

"He's from *Brazil*, Al. I told you that," I said.

"Didn't you say that was the same thing?"

"No, Al. I didn't. It's a whole 'nother country, remember?" Al had smoked so much dope in his lifetime, I was sure it'd fried his brain.

"Wherever he from, he play like a brother."

"If it's any consolation, his mother is half-black."

"Sho' nuff?" Mama said. "I didn't know there were black people in Brazil."

"Yes, ma'am. There are quite a few black people in Brazil," I replied.

Victor tugged on my hand and Mama and Aunt Nancy "oh'd" and "ah'd" all over themselves as he led me to the middle of the room.

"No one else is dancing, Victor. And besides, this is a kid's party," I whispered as he took me into his arms.

"The kids are outside," he replied.

"Okay, but like I said, there's no one else dancing."

"Music is playing and when there is music playing, someone must dance," he whispered back.

I rested against his body. "And that someone just has to be you?"

"Why not me?" he replied into my ear and then kissed it softly.

"Victor…"

He moved to my neck, caressed it with his finger, and kissed it gently. Then he gazed at me with a lopsided grin on his face. "Hmmm?"

"We're in a room full of people."

"I know." He backed away from me a bit and then leaned in and kissed me deeply, seeming to both resuscitate me and drain me of energy at the same time. My eyes darted around the room when he finally released me. Everyone in the room, and I mean *everyone,* was staring at us. Farrah's mouth was hung so low, I half-expected her tongue to slide out and hit the floor. Mama and Aunt Nancy were holding their chests and smiling at us.

As Victor pulled me closer and continued to dance, I smiled. No matter the circumstances of our union, it felt good to be Mrs. Victor Castro.

14

"Can't Let Go"

After three months of marriage, I heard words that were music to my ears: "Congratulations, you're pregnant."

According to the doctor, I was exactly three months along, putting the time of conception at our wedding night. Victor knew what he was talking about on that airplane. I thanked him about a hundred times, hugged him like I'd won an Oscar when the doctor gave us the news. He would never know how much I appreciated him.

After my breakups with Quincy, I never thought I'd know what carrying a child felt like. But there I sat in my comfy home, a real baby growing in my body and in just six months, I would be able to hold that baby in my arms. I felt good, and other than having less energy, I didn't feel any different physically at all. I was so happy.

I have to say that my first three months of marriage had been wonderful. Victor remained a complete gentleman. He was kind to me, and he worked diligently to get me pregnant. He cooked authentic Brazilian meals, let his hands work their magic on me whenever I asked, and accompanied me to church and social functions. He was by my side day and night, only leaving to go to the store or the gym. He was an excellent husband, so much so that most of the time I forgot he'd signed a contract. He even seemed happy to be with me, and he made me feel so loved that I sometimes forgot he didn't really love me. Sometimes I even felt that maybe I loved him.

So when I went to answer a knock at the front door, I was

smiling. At that point I didn't think things could get any better. "Who is it?" I called through the door, unable to see anyone through the peep hole.

"Delivery for Alex Weaver," said a weird voice.

I opened the door to find Quincy on the other side on bended knee—a bouquet of roses in one hand, a ring box in the other. My mouth dropped open. *Huh?* I hadn't talked to him since the day I called him about the lawyer. That was five months ago, and he had to know I was married. If Farrah hadn't thrown it in his face by now, surely someone else had told him. Victor and I had been seen together all over town. He *had* to know.

I frowned a little. "Um, Quincy? What are you doing?"

He smiled. "Look, it's been months, and I've given you your space, but I miss you, Alex. I'm ready, *really* ready, to give you what you want. Will you marry me, baby?"

"Um, Quincy, I'm married now... to someone else."

"I heard about that, and I want you to know that I forgive you. "

"Forgive me? Are you out of your mind? Forgive me for what?"

"For making a mistake and marrying someone you don't love. I figure by now you're looking for a way out, and I'm here to give it to you. I love you, and I know you love me. I forgive you, baby, and I'm ready to take the next step with you. Marry me."

"Quincy, I—"

"Who's at the door?" Victor asked as he walked into the foyer and stood behind me. He placed his hands on my shoulders and began to gently massage them.

Quincy stared at us for a moment before standing to his feet and squaring his shoulders. "Is this him?"

I nodded. "Quincy, this is my husband, Victor. Victor, this is... uh, a friend of mine, Quincy."

"Oh, I see. Well you should come in and celebrate with us," Victor said, much to my chagrin.

I smiled. "Oh, no, that's okay. Quincy was just leaving."

"What y'all celebrating, Alex?" Quincy asked.

"Did Alexandria not tell you? We're having a baby. Our first." He reached around and rubbed my stomach. Then he leaned in and softly nibbled my neck. I jumped.

Quincy wore a stricken expression as he backed away a little and shook his head. "A baby? Alex, what are you *doing*? You don't know him! You *can't* love him!"

I glanced at Victor and whispered, "Can you give us a moment?"

He shrugged, gave me a peck on the cheek, and backed out of the doorway. "Okay, but hurry. The food is getting cold."

"Okay." I turned to face Quincy again. "Um, Quincy, I'm sorry if this comes as a shock to you, but it's been months. I assumed you'd gone on with your life."

"I... I did. Or at least I tried to after I heard about you getting married, but I love you, Alex. And I thought you loved me, too. But now you're... you're pregnant? By some stranger with an accent? This is not you. You don't do stuff like this. Why?"

"Why, what? Why did I marry him? Why am I pregnant?"

"Why are you ruining your life like this? You don't love him. I *know* you don't."

I sighed. "Well, Q, love is a fantasy. It always has been. *You* taught me that."

He frowned. "I *do* love you. You have to believe that."

"No... actually, I don't. And besides, what I do is not your problem. I'm a grown woman, and I make my own decisions. I decided to marry Victor, and I'm carrying his child—another decision I made. We are doing fine. I'm happy, Q. Just accept that and move on."

"I can't accept that the woman I love is making the biggest mistake of her life."

I folded my arms over my chest. "Then what would you have me do? Throw Victor out and let you back into my life? Pick up where we left off?"

He stepped closer to me and looked right into my eyes. "Yes."

"Because you love me so much?"

He nodded. "And because *you* love *me*."

I stood there for a moment. I couldn't deny that he made a good case. I did still love him and from time to time, I missed him. Eight years is a long time—too long for the feelings to just disappear overnight.

He placed his hand on my cheek. "I could say it a thousand times, but it wouldn't be enough. I'm sorry for what I did. I will spend the rest of my life regretting it. But please don't throw what we had away over one mistake." He leaned in and planted a feather-light kiss on my lips.

I looked up at him and felt the love he was conveying with his words and with his kiss. "You know, I believe you're sorry. I do. And maybe you do love me, but do you love me enough to raise another man's child?"

He frowned slightly. "You'd still have it if we got back together?"

It was my turn to frown. "Q, you know I've always wanted children more than anything in the world. Of course I'd still have it!"

He shook his head. "Then, no. I don't think I can do that."

I chuckled bitterly. "I didn't think so. Your love runs just as deeply as I thought it did." I backed into my house and slammed the door shut. Then I leaned against it and fought bitter tears. Why had I let him do that to me? Why did I let him waltz back into my heart only to break it again?

"He's gone?" Victor asked. I looked up to see him standing in the doorway that led from the foyer into the living room.

"Yes."

"You let him kiss you."

"I... I know. I'm sorry. I don't know why I let that happen."

He shrugged. "No need to apologize to me. After all, this is not a real marriage, is it?"

Something in his voice sounded strange, different. Victor was always laid-back, never seemed to get upset or have a care in the world, but he sounded strained—no, he sounded *angry*.

"I, uh..." I wasn't sure how to react.

"You always say it is important to keep up appearances, to appear as the happy couple, and then you let him kiss you right on the doorstep. I find that strange." His voice still held an angry tone.

"I... I know. It won't happen again. He won't be back."

He looked at me for a moment and said, "You still love him?"

I dropped my head. "I don't know."

"It does not matter if you do. We have a deal."

I looked back up at him. "I know that. I'm not trying to break it. I appreciate you for helping me."

"Helping you?" he scoffed.

"Yes. Thank you. I'm very grateful."

Victor walked into the foyer and grabbed the car keys.

As he breezed past me, I said, "Where are you going?"

He turned and looked at me, gently placed his hand on my stomach, and said, "Out."

And I watched him leave, confusion filling every inch of me.

***

A full bladder awakened me around two the next morning. When I climbed out of bed, I noticed that Victor's side was just as empty as it had been when I climbed into it the previous evening. For the duration of our short marriage, we'd barely been apart at all. I'd grown accustomed to feeling his warmth in my bed, smelling his scent, and hearing his soft snore. So it felt strange to climb back into an empty bed. I'd almost forgotten how it felt to sleep alone.

I lay there staring at the ceiling for thirty minutes, listening to the stillness of my house, unable to go back to sleep. I finally decided that if I wasn't going to sleep, maybe I could write. I walked through my house, down the stairs to my office, and fired up the computer. Okay, so I can admit I was a little worried about Victor. He wasn't from Houston. Shoot, he wasn't even from the USA. *He could be out there in trouble somewhere*, I thought. *Or he could be out there with some other woman*, an evil voice said. I decided to ignore the evil voice, and besides, why would I care if he was with another woman? My only concern was whether or not he used protection. Other than that, he could do whatever he wanted with whomever he wanted. I didn't care. Did I?

I sighed as the words began to effortlessly fill the page in front of me. Nothing like a little personal drama to fuel creativity. I clicked away at the keys for a solid hour, took a quick break to fix a glass of water, and then returned to my computer and my soon-to-be-due manuscript. When I heard the lock turn in the front door, I was a little startled. For a brief moment, I'd forgotten that Victor was gone. As he quietly walked through the foyer, I waited for him to pass my office doorway, and then I spoke.

"I tried to call you," I said.

He stopped in his tracks and turned to look at me. "I know."

I stood from my desk and moved a little closer to him. "Why didn't you answer?"

"I was busy."

I stood there and stared at him. He looked irritated, like he didn't want to be bothered. "Victor, are you upset with me?"

He chuckled softly, walked over to me, and kissed my cheek lightly. "Of course not, *querida*."

He always called me that when we were out and about, especially when we were around my family. He told me it meant "darling" or "dear" in Portuguese. But the way he said it this time felt much less than sincere.

"Who were you with? Another woman?" I asked before I could stop myself. "I hope you used protection. You still owe me another child, you know?"

He leaned in close, the smell of liquor on his breath. "Do not worry, Alexandria. I know my duties, and I'll fulfill them to the letter."

With that, he planted a sloppy kiss on my lips and left the room. I found it impossible to work after that and decided to have another go at trying to get some sleep. My bed was still empty when I made it to my bedroom. After a quick look around my house, I found Victor in one of the guest bedrooms, fast asleep. I went to bed alone, an inexplicable sense of sadness hovering over me.

15

"I Think I Love U"

"Thanks for having lunch with me, Gwin," I said as I took another sip of my iced tea.

Gwin reclined in her seat at the table and eyed me suspiciously. "Mm-hmm. You gon' tell me what's up or not?"

I took a bite of my salad, glanced at the patrons surrounding us in the restaurant, and said, "What are you talking about?"

"I'm talking about the fact that since the day you came back home *married*, you haven't had time for any lunch dates. Barely spend five minutes at a time on the phone with me. You and your mister have been inseparable, and out of the blue you call me wanting to do lunch. Is there, uh, trouble in paradise since you guys found out about the baby?"

I sighed. There was no fooling Gwin. "There was never any paradise, Gwin, remember? This was a business deal from the start."

"Coulda fooled me. As a matter of fact, I was beginning to think you lied about the whole marriage contract thing."

"Why would I lie about something like that?"

Gwin shrugged. "Maybe you fell head over heels in love and you were too embarrassed to admit it. I don't know. But the way you two are together, the way you touch each other and look at each other… seems like more than a business deal to me."

I stared down at my plate. "Victor is a very good actor."

"What about you? Have you been acting?"

"Q came by the other day," I said, dodging her question.

Gwin's eyes widened. "Really? What did he want?"

"He professed his love to me and proposed again."

"What?!" Gwin shrieked. "He's got to know by now that you're married!"

"He knows. He just doesn't care. He was trying to rescue me from my mistake of marrying Victor."

"That's what he said, huh?"

I nodded. "Yeah, and I almost fell for it, Gwin. As good as Victor is to me, I almost fell for Quincy's okey doke. I even let him kiss me. Now Victor's acting all distant. He's barely said two words to me since Quincy came over. I don't know what to do."

Gwin looked amused as she leaned across the table. "You two are in love."

"Who two?"

"You and Victor."

I rolled my eyes. "No, we're not. It's a business—"

She raised her hand. "I know, I know. It's a business deal. You keep saying that, but it ain't the truth."

"Really, Gwin? Now you're going to call me a liar to my face?"

Gwin pulled her napkin from her lap and placed it on the table. "Okay, let me break it down for you, because I know this is what you called me for. You love him. Maybe you didn't at first, but you do now. He loves you. I have a feeling he's loved you longer than you've loved him. *No one* is that good an actor. He was upset about Quincy, because he loves you and he felt a little slighted, maybe even disrespected. You two love each other, but neither one of you has sense enough to admit it."

I laid my fork down and with a raised eyebrow said, "Suppose you're right. If you were me, what would you do?"

"Tell him you love him. I mean, seriously, what do you have to lose? You're already married to the man!"

"What if you're wrong? What if he doesn't love me or care about me at all?"

"Alex, do you realize how ridiculous you sound? You're sitting here afraid to tell your *husband* that you love him. Do you see the irony in this?"

"Come on, Gwin, don't do that."

"Do what?"

"Judge me. I already told you. I thought I was doing the right thing. I wanted a family."

She smiled. "And you wanted love and… it seems you've got everything you wanted."

I stared at her for a moment. "I can't ask him how he feels, Gwin. I just can't."

"Really? Big, bad, butt-kicking Alex Weaver is afraid to speak her mind? I can't believe it."

"Believe it. I'm petrified that he'll reject me."

She reached for my hand. "Then I suggest you do what you should've done long before you married him."

"What's that?"

"Pray."

Well, I couldn't argue with that.

She leaned forward and lowered her voice. "Now," she said. "Let me tell you what I heard the other day…"

And the gossiping began.

***

I prayed and prayed and tried to figure out what to do, but that was nearly impossible since I really didn't know how I felt. And I had committed so many sins—years of fornicating with Quincy followed by fornicating with Victor—I was unsure if God could hear me, anyway. Victor got over his anger, I guess, because he went right back to being the doting, attentive husband I'd grown accustomed to. And so there we were, back to our prior arrangement. An arranged, loveless marriage. And for the first time in a long time, I began to truly regret my decision to marry him. Because the possibility of being involved in a one-sided love affair was more unbearable to me than the idea of having never gotten married or never having kids.

We were sitting in the living room watching a movie together, one evening. I was sitting on my side of the couch, the side I sat on so often that the cushion had molded to perfectly accommodate my bottom. Victor was right beside me, one arm on the arm of the sofa, the hand of the opposite arm resting on my stomach. He laughed at something that happened on the movie I wasn't paying attention to and then glanced over at me. I smiled at him and rested my hand on top of his.

"When do you think I'll be able to feel the baby move?" he asked.

"Any day now, I guess. I'm almost four months along."

He leaned over and kissed my stomach. Then he rested his cheek against it and stayed there for a moment. Before I could stop myself, I reached down and gently rubbed my hand across his hair. He looked up at me and our eyes locked, and for a very brief moment, I said everything I ever wanted to say to him through my eyes. And in his eyes, I could read his feelings.

"Victor," I whispered. "I need to tell you something."

"What is it, querida?" he said, his voice soft—almost vulnerable.

"I... I'm afraid to tell you."

He sat up to face me. "You love me?"

I nodded slightly.

"You should not love me. I am no one to love, Alexandria."

I frowned slightly. "Why would you say something like that? What does that even mean?"

"Your love is precious, and you should not waste it on me."

"Victor, I don't know if this is some kind of Brazilian thing or something, but here in the US, you tell a person how *you* feel when they reveal something like this to you."

He stared at me for a long while. I searched his eyes, tried to see if they were speaking to me again. They were, but this time, all they would reveal to me was pain. A pain that I'd never seen in them before.

Victor stood from the couch. "It does not matter how I feel, Alexandria. What matters is that you cannot love me."

I looked up at him, confusion battling with despair inside of me. "Why?"

"Because this is the way it has to be. You should never forget what I was before we were married, what I really am. I *cannot* forget. I can never forget."

He left the room, and after sitting there on the sofa looking and feeling like a fool, I left and climbed the stairs. I noticed a light on in one of the guest bedrooms and when I made it to the doorway, found Victor lying in the bed fast asleep. I sighed as I made my way down the hall to my bedroom and after climbing into bed, I fell into a troubled sleep.

16

"I Wish I Wasn't"

The only thing running through my mind over the next months was: *I knew I shouldn't have told him. I knew it. I knew it. I knew it.*

In the months following my revelation, Victor moved out of my bedroom, didn't touch me even once, and barely spoke to me in passing. He spent most of his time at the gym working out or working, period, since he now had a job there… as a massage therapist. He left early in the morning, came home late at night, and I felt even more alone than I had before I married him.

If nothing else, though, his behavior helped me to focus on my work. I finished my novel and sent it to my editor in record time. But still, now, more than ever, I knew that marrying him had been a mistake. Oh, sure, he maintained the happily married front in public. He never missed a beat when we were out at a function, but the difference was that I knew for sure it was an act. I knew he didn't care about me, and it felt horrible.

The only person I'd confided in was Gwin, and her advice was to make him talk to me. To make him explain his transformation. But I didn't see any use in that. Why would I want to sit and listen to him tell me how he didn't love me? I'd have to be some kind of glutton for punishment to do that. So we went on living separate lives in the same house, and all I could do was pray for a quick second pregnancy so that the contract would be fulfilled and I could move on with my life without him.

I was eight months along when Gwin threw me a surprise baby

shower in her church's fellowship hall. It was the first day in a long while that I was able to genuinely smile. I didn't even let Farrah's presence upset me, because, to be honest, I was over her and what she did to me. I couldn't have cared less about her being there, but her constant leering at Victor was a little irritating. But Victor was Victor, and he made sure to put on a good show. He sat by my side, held my hand, rubbed my back, and kissed my cheek. He fixed my plate and handed me gifts and smiled and thanked everyone, and if I didn't know I was living with Mr. Hyde behind closed doors, I would've believed I was just as blessed as everyone kept gushing to me that I was.

When Victor handed me a huge box wrapped in lovely, expensive-looking paper, I noticed that Farrah moved to the front of the crowd of party attendees. She was wearing this weird smirk on her face and I wondered if the gift was from her. And if so, was it some sort of gag gift or something? Was something going to jump out of that box and bite me when I opened it? I quickly dismissed those thoughts. Not even Farrah was that immature.

Victor searched the outside of the box and said, "No tag, querida."

"Oh, well, maybe there's a card inside," I replied.

Victor ripped the paper off of the box, and I watched as he opened it to reveal a really nice bassinet complete with a sheet set. It was one of the things I had been planning to buy for the baby. It was actually on my gift registry, but it was so expensive, I never expected anyone to really buy it. "Wow," I said. "This is beautiful!"

"Here's the card," Victor said, handing me a pink envelope.

I opened it and read it aloud: *"A beautiful gift for what is sure to be a beautiful little girl. Congratulations, Alex. I'm glad you finally have what you've always wanted. I'm just sorry I can't be a part of your joy. I love you and I always will. Q."*

The room fell silent and stayed that way until Farrah spoke. "Quincy asked me to bring that to you. I hope you don't mind."

Before I could tell her to get out, Victor stood from his chair and stormed out of the room. My first instinct was to go after him. Why, I don't know, since he'd been little more than a roommate to me for months. Nevertheless, I excused myself and hobbled out of the room. Out of the corner of my eye I could see Gwin approaching Farrah. I was pretty sure my bestie was about to throw her trifling tail out.

I followed Victor all the way out to the parking lot. "Victor! Where are you going?!"

He stopped at my car and unlocked the door without acknowledging my question.

"Are you leaving me here?" I asked as I finally caught up with him and rested a hand on his arm.

He looked at me. "Yes."

"Why? Are you upset about Quincy's gift? I can send it back to him. I don't want anything from him."

"Are you sure, Alexandria?"

"What does that even mean? Are you jealous of Quincy, Victor?"

He leaned against the car. "Why would I be?"

I threw up my hands. "I don't know! What I do know is that you are confusing the heck out of me. You find out that I love you, and you distance yourself from me. You won't even talk to me unless we're in a room full of people. But if even a hint of Quincy surfaces, you get angry. I don't understand!"

"You do not understand that I am fulfilling the terms of our agreement? Is that not what you want me to do? Stay in character, play the role of a good husband? Is that not what the contract states?"

"Forget the contract. I wasn't sure before, but I am now. You love me, Victor, but you won't let yourself show it."

"You have no idea how I feel!" he yelled.

I slapped my hand against the hood of the car. "Then tell me!"

"I cannot love you, Alexandria. You are my employer and nothing else. Just... let's just have this baby and make another one so that we can go on with our lives."

"That's seriously what you want, Victor? That's how you want things to be?"

He reached down and caressed my cheek. "This is how things *must* be. I need to leave. Can Gwin take you home?"

I dropped my eyes and turned back towards the building. What was the use? "Sure. Why not?"

17

"Love Is A Losing Game"

Ruby Nell Weaver-Castro was born on a rainy Sunday evening. Victor was right by my side for the entirety of the labor. He held my hand and kissed my cheek and was thrilled to cut the cord. When the doctor handed her to him, he literally melted, and I could see that there was nothing he wouldn't be willing to do for her.

During the birth and the weeks that immediately followed, Victor lavished so much love and affection on me and little Ruby that I thought surely I'd died and gone straight to heaven. I don't even think it was because his mother flew in and spent two weeks with us, or because my entire family visited off and on. What he gave us was genuine, and the evidence of that was in the way he held me at night when no one else was around and the way he touched me and the way he looked at me. It was in his voice when he spoke to me. The way he moved back into my bedroom, and after the doctor released me, he showed me in the way he gave himself to me.

Then, as suddenly as he had turned back to me, he turned away from me again. When Ruby was three months old, I became pregnant with our second child, and as soon as I gave the news to Victor, he grew cold and once again, became little more than a roommate to me. He completely closed himself off from me. That's when I realized the affection and attention had been an act. *All of it*. It was only his way of ensuring fulfillment of our agreement—of speeding things along so that he could be rid of me once and for all. And that realization hurt me more than anything Quincy or Farrah had ever done to me.

The realization of being used bypassed my heart and pierced my very soul. And then there were the late nights and him crawling into bed with me smelling of another woman's perfume. There was his indifference towards Ruby whom he'd once adored. There were the nights he pulled me to him and touched me with the hands of a lover only to ignore me the next day. Those nights were the worst, because those nights I not only resented Victor, I also resented myself for being too weak to resist him. I hated myself for needing him, for loving him.

And so, the months passed by. My love and hatred for him grew in sync. The nights grew later and later until one night, he didn't come home at all. He didn't show up the next morning either. But after a week's absence, Victor returned to my house and my bed. And I found myself unable to contain my hurt and my fury any longer. My wounded heart was filled to the rim with pain. As soon as I felt him slip into bed next to me, I snatched the covers off of both of us and turned the lamp on. I glared at him as he lay there motionless, feigning sleep.

"Get the hell up!" I shouted.

Victor's eyes popped open, filled with surprise. "What's wrong?" he asked.

"What's wrong? Are you serious? I haven't seen or heard from you in a flippin' week! I've been in this house alone and seven months pregnant with another baby to take care of, and you haven't even had the common decency to call and say 'dog kiss my ass' or nothing!"

He sat up in the bed and gave me a confused look. "Why would I call you and say that?"

"It's a figure of speech, Victor. What I mean is you didn't even bother to check on me and Ruby for a whole week! What kind of man are you? Or is it just that terrible being married to me? Am I that undesirable to you? Do you despise me that much? Is it... is it my size? The way I look?" As soon as I released those words I wanted to reel them back in. No, no, no! This was all wrong! I was supposed to cuss him out and then put him out of my house. These pregnancy hormones were messing everything up! Then came the tears. This confrontation was turning into a mess.

For a second the old Victor was back. I could see it in his eyes—the love and compassion.

"Victor, I'm just trying to love you and be with you. I don't understand why you keep doing this. Sometimes we're so good together, and then you start to change and it's so frustrating to me. And it hurts. I'm tired of being hurt!"

"Alexandria, loving me was not part of the deal. I never asked you to love me, and you never asked me to love you," he said softly.

"Love is not something you can plan for and put in a contract. It just happens. I know you feel the same, or at least that's how it seems sometimes."

"Querida, I told you, there is business and then there is pleasure. You are trying to mix the two, and that is never a good thing."

"What? I don't want to hear that business/pleasure mess right now! My heart is breaking. Do you not care at all?"

He closed his eyes and shook his head. "Stop loving me. That should fix your heart."

"That doesn't make any sense. I can't just erase how I feel."

He sighed. "Alexandria..."

"Do you love me, Victor?"

Silence.

"Do you?!"

"It does not matter."

"It does to me!" I shouted.

"You're going to wake the baby."

"As if you care about the baby! As far as I can see, all you care about is yourself and money and whoever you're sneaking around with. Are you in love with someone else?"

"No!"

"But there is someone else, isn't there?"

Silence.

"Are they paying you?"

More silence.

"You are a coward, and I hate you! Forget the contract. I'll pay you for your services. But I want you to get out of here and never come back again!"

He moved towards me and tried to pull me to him. "Querida…"

I snatched away from him and climbed out of the bed. "Don't *querida*, me! Get away from me. I'm not letting you sex me into submission again!"

"Calm down. Think about the baby." He stood from the bed, walked over to me, and then leaned in and kissed me. For a second I forgot I was angry, but I quickly came back to myself.

"No! You're not going to do this again," I said as I backed up towards the doorway. "I want you to pack your stuff and get out! Go be with her, whoever she is. Let her foot your bills, and stay away from me and my children!"

He stepped forward. "Alexandria..."

I picked up a lamp and threw it at him. "No! Get out!"

"I'm sorry."

I walked to the closet and began to yank his clothes off the hangers and fling them at him. "Get out! Get out! Get out!"

The baby whimpered, and Victor left the room. I followed him into the nursery. "Don't touch my baby!" I shrieked, startling Ruby, whose cries grew louder.

He cradled her in his arms. "It's okay, little one," he said calmly.

"Give her to me," I said with an unsteady voice. "Give her to me, and get out."

"Okay, I'll leave if you want me to leave. But I am not giving her to you until you calm down."

"What?! Give me my baby now, you worthless piece of—give her to me, Victor, and get out!!"

"No."

That was it. The rage took over, and I think I forgot for a second that he was holding Ruby. All of the pain inside of me—the pain from Quincy and Farah and from my hired husband—spewed out at once. I picked up a container of baby powder and hit him over the head with it while shouting, "Put her down!" A cloud of fragrant white billowed around us.

I'd startled him. He looked at me and backed away a little. "You would hit me while I am holding our child?"

"Get out!"

He slowly laid Ruby in her crib, and she kicked her crying up another notch. But I couldn't do anything about that at the moment. As soon as she was out of his arms, I jumped him, slapping and hitting him anywhere I could. I screamed and fought, and all the while, he struggled to get away from me. He never hit me back, and I think that upset me more than anything. I clawed at his beautiful face and pulled his gorgeous hair until, finally, he managed to get a grip on my arms to stop me.

"Alexandria, stop! I'll go. I'll go now!"

He let me go, and I leaned against a wall, breathing exhausted, heaving breaths. I looked over at Ruby, who was hoarse and red-faced, and picked her up to calm her. Victor had moved to leave the room when the doorbell rang.

"I'll get it," I said. "You just need to pack your mess and get out of here."

I made my way down the stairs to the front door and yelled "Who is it?"

"Police!"

I snatched the door open, forgetting that I was wearing only a nightshirt. "Yes?"

The officer's eyes widened as he looked at me, and I realized how I must've looked at that moment. After all, I'd just spent the last twenty minutes assaulting my husband.

"Can I help you, officer?"

"Yes, ma'am. Is everything okay here? We got a call about a disturbance."

I opened my mouth to speak, but Victor, who was now standing behind me, said, "We're sorry, officer. This is embarrassing, but we were just making love, sir."

The officer frowned. "The person who called it in said it sounded like a fight."

Victor rested his hand on my shoulder. "Yes, my wife can be very passionate. So can I."

"And that's how you got those scratches on your face? She was being passionate?"

"Yes..."

"Sir, are you sure everything is okay in here?"

"Everything is fine. We're sorry for any trouble."

"Ma'am?" The officer said, his eyes glued to me.

"Uh... yes, we're fine. Sorry."

"Okay, well, try to keep it down in here. Beautiful baby, by the way."

"Thank you," Victor said; then he reached around me and closed the door.

"Why'd you lie for me?" I asked.

"Because you do not belong in jail. What happened here is my fault, but I'll leave now. It will be better for you."

"You're leaving?"

"Yes. Is that not what you wanted? Is that not why you beat me up?"

"I didn't beat you up. I just... you hurt me, Victor. I needed you, and you hurt me."

"Do you want me to leave? Tell me what you want me to do, and I will do it. After all, you are the boss."

I closed my eyes. "Don't say that. I just want you to be here with me, to hold me and love me."

"I cannot do that."

"No, you don't *want* to do it."

"Alexandria, I am a whore, or did you forget that? I use women for money. Anything I say or do to a woman is for money. I lie to them. This is what I do. It is all I am good at. Even if I stand here and tell you that I love you. Even if I mean it, I will hurt you one day, because it is my nature to do so. It seems I have already hurt you. So we will have this new baby and then we will divorce. You will pay me, and I will move on to my next client."

"That's it? That's all you have to say? I'm just a client?"

"Yes."

I pulled my hand back to slap him, but he grabbed my arm tightly and stopped me. "No more hitting, yeah? I'll go now." He turned his back on me.

"I love you, Victor. Just please tell me. Do you love me at all?"

He faced me, dropped his eyes, and said, "There are feelings there, Alexandria."

"Feelings for me?"

He nodded. "Yes."

"Feelings of love?"

"It does not matter, querida," he said, then grabbed a duffel bag full of some of his things and left on foot.

I ended up spending the night on the floor in the nursery, unable to sleep. What had I done to my life? What was I thinking, believing that I could arrange the perfect life? I'd been so blinded by my desire to have a family, I didn't think about the consequences of how I'd gone about doing it. In my selfishness, I'd given my children a distant father and a brokenhearted mother. I just didn't count on things going this way. It never occurred to me when I was drafting the contract and working out the details that I would actually fall in love with Victor. I never once thought that I'd end up right where I began in the first place—with a shattered heart.

Had I known this was how I'd end up, I would've just stuck with Quincy. After all, Farrah wasn't really pregnant. And she was back in my life anyway. I didn't even really want to kill her anymore, and maybe I still loved Quincy.

Maybe.

As I lay there with the sun streaming in through the window, listening to Ruby's soft breathing as she slept and rubbing my hand across my growing stomach, I sincerely poured my heart out to God in prayer, for only His guidance could help me now.

18

"On And On"

I spent the next two weeks in my house, refusing to answer my phone or my door. In one word, I was depressed. Depressed and hurt and angry at myself more than I was at Victor. In marrying Victor, I thought I was taking control of my life and my future, but as it turned out, I wasn't in control of anything, least of all my emotions. It seemed that my heart and soul wanted the real thing—a real love and a real marriage, yearned for it even though my mind didn't think I needed it.

So I sat in my living room with Ruby in her swing and watched as she rocked back and forth… back and forth. I stared at her and imagined I was someone else, somewhere else. I imagined my life wasn't a total mess and I hadn't fouled it up by making dumb, rushed decisions. I pretended I wasn't going to have to raise my children alone. I pretended I wasn't behind on writing my next book. I pretended my heart hadn't been shot full of holes. I pretended I didn't love a man who didn't—no, *wouldn't* love me back.

I closed my eyes and prayed for the hundredth time for the strength to forget Victor and as he'd put it, to stop loving him. In the midst of my prayer there was a knock at the door. I ignored it and kept right on praying. Imagine my shock when I heard a key turn in the lock. I sat up straight and for a second, wondered if it was Victor. Then I went into a mental tailspin, thinking about how horrible I must've looked at that moment. Then I admonished myself for being so excited at the thought of Victor returning home. Home? I really was losing my mind. This had never been his home.

Nevertheless, I smoothed my hand over my hair, kicked the wet diapers under the ottoman, and waited for him to enter the living room. To my surprise, it was Gwin who entered the room, and right behind her was Quincy. Now I was really embarrassed. I pulled a throw over my legs and tried to recall the last time I'd bathed.

"I don't know why you looking all surprised. You haven't answered your phone in over a week. I was worried to death, and Lord help your mama," Gwin said as she took a seat next to me.

I shrugged and dodged Quincy's eyes which were glued to me. "I didn't feel like talking."

"Are you all right?" Quincy asked softly.

"Yes, why wouldn't I be?" I answered defensively.

"One of my buddies on the police force called me a couple of weeks ago and said they'd received a call about a disturbance at your address. I wanted to check earlier, but I didn't want you to feel like I was trying to get in your business. So I decided to call Gwin to check on you, and she said she couldn't get in touch with you. I just… I got worried," he said with genuine concern in his voice.

I stared at him for a moment. Standing there in his suit with what looked like a fresh haircut, he looked like *my* Quincy. The one I'd fallen in love with. The one I was supposed to marry. There was no sense in denying the fact that he looked good. And I still felt that little tug on my heart I always felt when I was around him. I guess I still loved him. But how could that be when I loved Victor? Didn't I love Victor?

"Thanks for your concern. Both of you," I finally said. "But I'm fine. *We're* fine."

"Where's your husband?" Gwin asked.

With wide eyes I said, "He's not here."

Quincy shifted on his feet. "Did he hurt you? Is that what the disturbance was about?"

I motioned toward the loveseat. "You can sit down if you want."

He nodded and plopped down on the loveseat. "Did he hurt you, Alex?" he repeated.

"No, he didn't. Look, I'm glad you came to check on me, Quincy, but—"

He held up his hand. "But you don't want to discuss your marriage with me here. I understand." He stood and peered down at Ruby. "She's beautiful, Alex. Just like her mother."

I gave him a small smile. "Thanks, Quincy."

"If you need me, call. Number hasn't changed."

"Okay."

"I mean it, Alex."

I nodded slightly. "I know."

He left, closing the front door softly behind him. And Gwin wasted no time pouncing on me.

"What happened?" she asked.

I rehashed the events of the night I threw Victor out of the house, ending with, "You were right. I made a huge mistake, and I've made a mess of my life, Gwin. I just don't know what to do now." I felt tears spring into my eyes.

Gwin sighed. "Well, I'm not here to say 'I told you so.' I'm here to help you. So the first thing we're gonna do is clean this joint up. I'll handle that while you go take a shower, because you are tart, girl."

I tried to frown but couldn't help laughing, because she was definitely right. I smelled like a patch of wild onions right at that moment. She laughed, too. Then my laughter morphed into tears, and she grabbed me and pulled me into a comforting hug.

"You're gonna be all right. You're gonna get cleaned up, and then you're gonna write that new book even if I have to move in here and become Ruby's nanny. You're gonna make it, Alex."

I nodded and sniffled. "I've been praying so hard, Gwin. I feel so lost and so stupid, thinking that I could have a real love and a real marriage with a gigolo. I just wanted something real for once."

She released me and cupped my face in her hands. "You had something real, Alex. Quincy was real. He's *still* real."

I shook my head. "I can't think about Quincy in that way anymore. Soon I'll have two children by Victor, and Quincy's already made it clear that he won't raise another man's kids. I'll just have to go it alone. I'll manage, I guess."

"I think you're underestimating Quincy."

"I know what I heard him say out of his own mouth."

"Okay. Look, will you do me a favor, Alex?"

"Sure."

"Will you come to church with me this Sunday?"

I smiled. That was just the invitation I needed. If I needed anything at that moment, it was some Jesus. "Yes. I haven't been in a couple of months. I never used to miss church."

"I know. I think it's about time you got back in there."

"Yeah, me, too."

***

I was glad to be attending service at Gwin's church instead of my own. I could imagine the side-eyed looks and murmurs my entrance would garner at my own church—especially since I'd be minus Victor. I'd only been to Gwin's church a couple of times before, and thankfully, the membership was large and easy to blend into. No one even seemed to notice me or my huge belly as we weaved through the crowd in the foyer, making our way to the sanctuary. We took a seat on a pew near the rear of the mega church, and I felt a little of the weight that had been on my shoulders lighten.

I looked over at Ruby sitting in Gwin's lap in her frilly pink dress and then felt the baby inside of me move and thought to myself that my children were truly blessings to me—no matter how they came to be in my life. They were the best part of me and the best part of Victor. They were not a mistake even if the marriage was. They were planned, and I would make sure they knew that.

I smiled and watched as the sanctuary rapidly filled with worshippers. A few seconds before service began, I felt someone sit down beside me on the pew, and when I turned to speak to them, my smile faded, and it took everything in me not to elbow Gwin in the ribs. There beside me, looking exceptionally good, was Quincy. He gave me a little smile and said "hi." But before I could say a word to either him or Gwin, service began.

As the melodic voices of the choir filled my ears, I quickly forgot about Gwin's and Quincy's little ambush. For just a little while, I even forgot about how I had ruined my life. For two whole hours, I thought about and felt nothing but the goodness of God. I let the praises sung by the choir sink into my soul, and I allowed the words of the sermon to flow into my heart. The pastor spoke about second chances. He said that God was faithful and that what He has for us is always for us. We need only seek Him and obey Him to see his plan for our lives come to fruition. With God, it's never too late. He is always waiting for His child to return to Him. He will always welcome us home.

Being there and hearing that message helped me to clear some of the cobwebs from my mind. And when service was over, I didn't feel so hopeless anymore.

As I stood and gathered my purse and diaper bag, Quincy, who hadn't breathed a word throughout the entire service, said, "That was some message, huh?"

I nodded and gave him a polite smile. "Yes, I really got a lot out of it."

"Me, too. Um, Alex, would you have lunch with me?"

I glanced at Gwin, who was pretending to check Ruby's diaper. "Um, now?" I asked.

"Well… yes. My treat, of course."

"Um… I'd have to switch the car seat over from Gwin's car to yours, and that is really a hassle, and I don't want to hold Gwin up."

"I'll switch it over if you tell me what to do," Quincy said.

"And you're not holding me up. My Sundays are for me. My hubby knows not to expect me home anytime soon. That's the price he has to pay for refusing to attend church with me. And besides, once you take the car seat, I'm heading to the mall to get some shopping in, and I don't have to be there at a certain time," Gwin chimed in.

"Shopping alone? Really?" I asked. I knew she was lying.

"Girl, yes! I do my best shopping alone. You two go ahead and enjoy your lunch."

I sighed and found myself out of excuses. "Okay."

All three of us filed out to the parking lot—Gwin with Ruby on her hip. It took only a little instruction for Quincy to remove Ruby's car seat from Gwin's Lexus and install it in his Mercedes. In no time, I was sitting in his front seat as he drove through the city to my favorite barbecue joint.

He parked the car, hopped out, and opened the door for me. "You remembered?" I asked, nodding toward the restaurant.

He smiled. "How could I forget?"

I freed Ruby from her seat, and the three of us headed into the restaurant, almost looking like a family. And that's when the sadness hit me. We *should've* been a family. Ruby should've been Quincy's daughter, not Victor's. And then the shame and despair returned as I was reminded of the mistakes I'd made.

Lunch was quiet as those troubling thoughts that were only temporarily silenced during the church service screamed in my mind.

"You okay?" Quincy asked, picking up on the change in my mood.

I closed my eyes and for a second thought about lying. But then I realized I was tired of lying and pretending. My entire life since marrying Victor had been a lie, and I just did not have the energy to keep up the performance.

"No, I'm not, Q," I said softly.

He reached across the table and rested his hand on top of mine.

"You can tell me."

I looked up at him, at the sincere expression on his face. "There's too much to tell right now."

"Take your time. Tell me a little today and some more tomorrow and then more the next day, until you get it off of your chest."

"Why?" I asked as I lifted Ruby from the high chair and sat her in my lap.

"Why, what?"

I shrugged. "Why do you care? It's been a long time since we were together. I'm married, now. I have a child and another one on the way, and neither of them is yours. You've already made it clear that you don't want to raise another man's children, and I know you've moved on with your life by now. So, why?"

He sighed and leaned back in his seat. "I still love you, Alex. I mean, sure, I've been with other women since we split up. But none of them were you. You're special, and I'll never forgive myself for messing things up with you, for hurting you. I'm sorry, Alex. But more than that, it hurts me to think that you're hurting now. That another man hurt you. I feel like it's my fault. Those should be my children, not his."

I shook my head. "Nothing is your fault. I made my own decisions—good or bad."

"But I hurt you, and I can't help but think that had something to do with your decision to marry some guy you barely knew."

I looked down at Ruby, who looked so much like her father. "I'll admit that I was desperate. I wanted a family, and I felt like my only chance to have one disappeared with the end of our relationship. So when I met Victor and we... hit it off, I thought he was the answer to my prayers."

Quincy leaned forward and raised an eyebrow. "But he wasn't?"

"There's no simple answer for that question. In some ways, he was. For a while, he was very good to me. He made me feel wanted and desirable at a time when I was very low. What you did with Farrah shot a lot of holes in my self-esteem, you know? And plus, he gave me Ruby, and soon I'll have another child."

Quincy's eyes dropped, and he softly cleared his throat.

"I'm sorry. Am I making you uncomfortable?"

He shook his head. "No, no, continue, please."

I bit down on my bottom lip. "I thought I had everything figured out. I mean, even if things didn't work out, at least I could say I'd once been married, and at least I'd have my kids. But I was wrong. That's not enough. It was never enough."

"What do you mean?"

"I mean, I didn't account for the lack of love or how it would affect me."

Quincy moved his hand and wiped invisible sweat from his brow. "Lack of love?"

I nodded. "I miss love. I miss having someone truly love me. Or at least the idea of someone loving me, since I'm not sure if I've ever had a man truly love me," I said. My transparency and openness with Quincy was a shock even to me.

With a creased brow, he said, "I truly loved you, Alex. I *still* do. I love you from the bottom of my heart, baby."

I could hear the sincerity in his voice, and I could feel the words of his confession in my soul. Tears began to crowd my eyes. "I want to believe that, Q. I really do."

He reached for my hand again, grasping it tightly. "Believe it, Alex. *I love you.*"

"Even now?"

"Yes."

I took a deep breath and quickly wiped away the single tear that managed to escape. "I wish things could be different."

"They *can* be. All we gotta do is try," he said softly.

"I love him, Q."

I could tell by the look on his face that my words had come as a surprise to him. "Oh… I see. Are you… you planning to reconcile with him?"

"No. He doesn't love me. He's made that painfully clear. I'm going to divorce him after this baby is born."

He was silent for a while. I sat in the booth opposite him and tried to figure out what to say next. He beat me to the punch. "Do you still love me at all, Alex?"

"Sometimes I think I do," I said honestly.

"Sometimes?"

"Yes, and sometimes I think I hate you. It's the same with Victor."

"I see. Do you think you could ever give me another chance, give *us* another chance?"

I tilted my head to one side. "Well, I can't really say no. I guess anything is possible. But my children are not going to disappear. And neither is Victor. I really want him to be in their lives."

"I understand that. I would never ask you to abandon your kids for me."

"Okay, so you say you love me. Do you think you could love my children?"

He paused for a second and then said, "I could try. I *want* to try,"

I smiled. "If you really mean that, where do we start?"

"We already have. I've enjoyed the meal and the conversation, and the baby is beautiful, Alex. I'm sure the next one will be, too."

"Thank you."

"You're welcome. Well, let me take you two home. If it's all right with you, I'd like to call you tomorrow."

"I think that'd be great."

When I walked through the front door of my home thirty minutes later, I felt something I hadn't felt in weeks—hope.

19

"I'm For Real"

I woke up the next morning with fresh inspiration and a new resolve to finish the latest installment of the Diva Chronicles. In this book, one of the ladies was actually falling in love and dealing with the fallout from her perpetually single friends. After checking on a still-sleeping Ruby, I plugged up my laptop, sat at the desk in my bedroom, and began to bang out page after page. Before I knew it, I had typed two whole chapters, finishing just in time to change and feed Ruby for the first time that morning. I was burping her when the doorbell rang. With Ruby on my hip, I answered it and, to my surprise, Quincy was standing there holding a bouquet of flowers and a stuffed polar bear.

I smiled as I backed out of the doorway and let him into the house.

"I woke up with you on my mind. I hope it was okay for me to drop by," he said as he followed me into the living room.

"Oh, well, sure. It's okay."

He handed me the flowers and the bear. "I hope she likes bears."

"Well, I don't know that she doesn't. Thank you for thinking of her. That was really sweet of you."

He sat down beside me on the sofa. "Um, you sure it's okay for me to be here? I mean your husband's not gonna come barging into the house and beat me up, is he?"

I shrugged. "You know, Q… to be honest, he left two weeks ago and I haven't seen him or heard from him since. I don't think he's too concerned about who I spend my time with."

Quincy's eyes widened. "Really? Two weeks? He must be out of his mind."

I adjusted Ruby in my lap. "I don't know. We'd been arguing, and things hadn't been good between us for a while before—never mind all that. What are you doing here in your jeans and t-shirt? No suit? No work today?"

He settled into his side of the sofa, the side he always sat on when we were together. "I took the day off."

"Why? You sick or something?"

He grinned. "Sick from missing you."

I rolled my eyes. "Whatever."

"No, I'm serious. Do you have any idea what life has been like for me since we split up? Dating women who could never compare to you. No one can make me feel the way you do, Alex."

I dropped my eyes. "How… how do I make you feel?"

"The way you loved me? Girl, I can't even really explain it except to say that no one, and I mean *no one,* has ever made me feel that way before or after you. It was never about what I could do for you. You're independent and smart. The only thing you wanted from me was my love, and I appreciated that. I miss you, Alex." He scooted closer to me, rubbed the back of his hand along my cheek. "I *need* you."

I felt the heat inside of me rise and slid a little further down the couch from him. "Q, I'm eight months pregnant. I've gained a million pounds on top of the million I already weighed, my feet are swollen, and my nose is the size of a Cadillac. I feel like a pregnant yak."

"You look absolutely beautiful to me."

"Are you trying to sleep with me?"

"Well, I ain't gonna lie. Motherhood looks good on you and it's turning me on, but I wouldn't ask you to do something like that while you're pregnant and still married. I know you've got morals. I always admired that about you."

"Humph, I didn't have enough morals not to sleep with you before marriage."

He smiled that smile that I always loved so much. "Well, I *am* irresistible, baby."

I shook my head. "Same old Q."

"The same one you fell in love with."

I met his gaze. "Yeah."

He reached over and touched Ruby's hand. "Can I hold her?"

I looked from him to Ruby. "Um… well, sure, if you want to."

I handed her to him and he held her in an awkward position, almost as if he was afraid he'd break her or something. Then he relaxed and sat her in his lap. He looked at me and smiled. "I think maybe she likes me. I mean she's not crying or anything."

I returned his smile. "She's got a really good disposition. She's a good baby."

Ruby gripped his finger in her little hand. "Yeah," he said through a wide smile. He began to gently bounce her on his knee. Ruby giggled lightly. "I see why you wanted her so badly. She's special."

"Yes, she is."

"I could… I could get used to this, you know?" he said, his eyes glued to Ruby.

I reached over and rubbed my hand over Ruby's hair. "Well, I think it's a good look for you, Q. I always thought you'd be a good father."

"Really?"

I nodded. "Yes. That's why I wanted to marry you so badly. That, and I also loved you very much."

He stood Ruby up in his lap and smiled at her. "If you let me try, I bet I can make you love me that much again."

I tilted my head to the side and inspected this handsome man who once made my heart flutter. "Q, can I tell you something?"

He sat Ruby back down in his lap. "Hey, what color are her eyes? They're so pretty."

"They're amber, like her father's. Q, did you hear me?"

"Yeah. I'm not sure I want to hear what you have to say, though. I really don't like being rejected," he said solemnly.

"I'm not going to reject you. I just need to tell you something."

"All right."

"Q, when we first got together, I thought it was a joke or something. I mean, there you were, this tall, handsome, immaculately-dressed, professional man, and you were asking *me* out."

He frowned. "Alex, what are you talking about? Of course I asked you out. I'm not dumb. I know a good catch when I see one."

I adjusted in my seat. "That's just it. I... I've always had these problems with my self-esteem. I didn't understand why a man like you would be interested in a woman who looks like me."

He wore a stunned expression. "Alex, baby, is there something wrong with your eyes? Are the mirrors in this place broken? You're beautiful. Can't you see that?"

I dropped my eyes and shook my head. "Sometimes, I can and sometimes, I can't. Sometimes, all I see is 200-plus pounds of fat and a chubby face and hair that won't ever do what I want it to do."

He faced me and stared into my eyes. "Alex, I love your body and your face and your hair. Hell, you can shave your head bald, and you'd still be attractive. Didn't your mother ever tell you how beautiful you are?"

I sat and meditated on his question for a moment. "Well, no, I don't guess she did. She always bragged about me being smart. It was Farrah who got all of the compliments on her looks, not me. Farrah got most of the attention, really."

"Well, she *should* have told you. Farrah's cute and she's small, but there's no substance there. She doesn't have any goals or direction. Baby, let me tell you; there's nothing sexier than a woman with goals. Intelligence turns me on like nothing else. You're the total package: brains *and* beauty."

"Well, thank you, Q. I can't deny that being with you made me feel pretty for the first time in my life. But there were these thoughts that were always in the back of my head. I was always waiting for the punch line. I almost felt like you were biding your time with me until something better came along."

"Did I do something to make you feel that way?"

I shrugged. "Well, yes and no. You were always good to me, but the fact that you refused to set a wedding date fueled my insecurities."

He handed Ruby to me, stood from the sofa, and began pacing the room. "*Wow*. I always thought you were confident. I mean, you never hesitated to speak your mind, and you were never the type to take any mess from anyone."

"That's just it, Q. By sitting around all of those years, sleeping with you, playing house with you—I was taking mess the whole time. I should've stood my ground, done what is right in the eyes of God, and stopped giving you my goodies for free."

He stopped in his tracks. "For free?"

I sat Ruby in her swing. "What I mean by that is I shouldn't have been laying up with you. I didn't give you any reason to think you *needed* to marry me."

He reclaimed his seat on the sofa. "I see. Well, I never meant to take advantage of you. I... I just didn't think I was ready for that kind of commitment."

"I just don't understand that, Q. I mean, was I the only woman in your life?"

"Yes."

"Did you love me?"

"Still do."

"Then you were already committed to me. What was so hard about making it official?"

He sighed. "I don't know. Marriage is... it's scary, Alex. You'd have to be a man to understand."

"I guess so."

"Look, I had no idea you had all of those feelings inside of you. I guess what happened between me and Farrah just made things worse. I'm sorry."

"I know you are. But what happened with her didn't necessarily make me feel worse. It made me feel like I was right all along, and a part of me was kind of relieved that it had finally happened."

We were both quiet as the words I'd spoken settled between us.

"Alex, can I tell you something?" Quincy finally said.

"Yes."

"I always felt like you were reliable. I guess I felt like you'd always be there with me and *for* me. I never really thought you'd leave me, and when you did, it shocked the hell out of me."

"I could tell you were a little upset."

"A little? I was *devastated*, baby. I didn't know what to do, but I knew I had to get you back."

"That's why you agreed to set a date?"

"Yes. I would've done anything you asked at that point."

"I wish you had just left things as they were. Instead, you agreed to do something you weren't ready to do. And you… you broke my heart, Q."

"I know I did, and I'm so sorry. I love you, Alex. I don't know how I can say it to make you believe it, but I do. I want to marry you and be a father to your kids. I can't promise I'll always know the right thing to say or do, but I promise from the bottom of my soul that I will never do anything to hurt you again. *I promise you that, baby.*"

I noticed there were tears in his eyes as I reached over and hugged him. "I believe you, Q. I believe you."

He backed away a little. "Will you give me another chance?"

I sighed. "I would love to. But there's something I need to tell you first, and it's something that might make you see me differently."

He shook his head. "Nothing could make me see you differently."

"We'll see about that." I took a deep breath and released it. "Victor is a gigolo, and I hired him to marry me and father my children."

"Say what?"

I stood from the sofa and crossed the room. "I said, Victor is a gigolo, and I hired him to marry me and father my children."

He was silent… speechless, I guess, and that's saying a lot for a lawyer.

"If this changes your mind about me, about us, I totally understand. But know that I was desperate when I made that decision. I didn't think I had any other options." I leaned against the wall and peered down at Ruby. "I just… I just wanted a family."

He dropped his head and clasped his hands in his lap. I watched as he took a deep breath and looked up at me. "I thought you said you loved him. Did you say that just to hurt me?"

"No, I… I *grew* to love him. He was very good to me, but I guess he was just doing his job."

Quincy nodded. "Well, Alex, I still love you. There's nothing you can say or do to change that, and if anything, I'm relieved to hear that your marriage wasn't real."

"Really?"

He stood and walked over to me. "Yes, *really*. Now I don't have to worry about him trying to hang around and get in our way. You can divorce him, and we can move on."

I closed my eyes in relief. "Thanks for not judging me."

"If you're willing to give us another chance after what I did, I have no right to judge you. Let's just put the past in the past, baby, and make the future greater. Okay?"

He pulled me tightly into his arms, and I said, "Okay."

20

"I Wanna Know"

A week before my due date, I received the phone call from Victor's mother. Quincy was on the floor playing with Ruby, who was crawling all over the place. When I saw her number on my screen, I was both surprised and apprehensive. I wasn't sure what I should or would say to her.

"Hello?" I said as I slipped out of the living room into the kitchen.

"Alexandria? Is Victor there?" she replied.

"Um… no, ma'am. He's not."

"Oh, my!" she said, sounding borderline hysterical. She broke into a string of Portuguese words I didn't understand. Then she spoke in English again. "I am so worried. I have not heard from him in three weeks. He usually calls me every Sunday. Is something wrong?"

Three weeks? He hadn't called his mother since we separated? Maybe he was just embarrassed. "Um, well, we had a fight, a *huge* fight, and he left… three weeks ago. I haven't heard from him either."

"What?! Where did he go?"

"I… I don't know, Mrs. Castro."

"Well, have you tried to call him? When I call, there is no answer."

I was beginning to feel a little embarrassed. I must've seemed like a horrible wife to her. "No, I haven't tried to call him."

"Has he not called you at all? Not even for Ruby? Not with the new baby on the way soon?"

I sat down at the kitchen table and lowered my head. "No."

"And you do not think something is wrong?"

"No, I… I *didn't*. This is not the first time he's been out of touch with me."

"Well, he has *never* missed a week of calling me! Not in Brazil, not in America. Never! Should I come there? I am very worried about him."

"No, no. I'll find him. I'll be sure to have him call you."

"Okay, thank you, Alexandria."

I sighed as I ended the call and laid my phone on the table. I held my head in my hands and stared down at the phone, then I picked it up, dialed Victor's number, and listened as it rang straight to voicemail.

"You okay?" Quincy asked.

I looked up to find him standing next to the table, holding Ruby. I shook my head. "No. It seems that Victor is missing," I said as I ended the call.

He frowned as he took a seat across from me. "Missing?"

"Yeah, no one's heard from him since he left here."

Quincy shrugged. "So?"

"So, that was his mother on the phone. She hasn't heard from him. I never should've let him leave like that. He was on foot, carrying a duffel bag. Anything could've happened to him."

"You're worried because he hasn't called his mother? I haven't talked to my mother in six months."

"Victor is different, Q. He and his mother are very close. He wouldn't miss calling her unless something was wrong."

"Okay…"

I picked up my phone. "I'm gonna call the police and file a missing person's report."

"Are you sure you should do that? I mean, maybe he just needs some time alone."

"That may be true, but if he's out there and something's happened to him, I'll never forgive myself for not trying to find him or help him. I mean, he's still my husband, and I did bring him here—far away from his home. Plus, he's the father of my children. I owe him that much."

"He's nothing more than hired help, Alex. You owe him nothing but payment for his services."

"Quincy—"

He held up a hand. "Never mind. Do what you gotta do."

I reached for his hand. "Look, this doesn't change anything. I'm still going to divorce him after this baby is born, and I'm still willing to work on us."

He nodded and stood from the table. "Go ahead and make your call. We'll be in the living room."

"Thank you, Q."

"No problem, baby."

I called the police and about an hour later, an officer arrived to take the report. I felt a little embarrassed when he asked why I'd waited three weeks, but I explained that we weren't getting along well and that he'd also been out of touch with other members of his family. The officer almost out and out dismissed me as being a hysterical pregnant woman, but I didn't care. At least I'd done my part. My conscience was clear.

Four days passed, and I was preparing for the upcoming birth of my second child when the police officer called me.

"Hello?" I said, my nerves on edge as I feared the worst possible news regarding Victor.

"Mrs. Castro? This is Officer Riley—Houston PD."

"Yes, do you have some news about my husband?"

Quincy, who was sitting on the side of my bed holding Ruby and watching me pack my suitcase, focused on me with anticipation in his eyes.

"Yes, ma'am. We've found him."

21

"Me and Mr. Jones"

I rushed through the house with Ruby on my hip as I waited for Gwin to arrive.

"You sure you don't want me to come with you?" Quincy asked.

"No, I'll be fine. I mean, I'm going to a hospital. If anything happens, they can just roll me into Labor and Delivery."

Quincy nodded. "I can keep Ruby. You didn't have to call Gwin."

"I know, and I appreciate the offer, but Gwin's just got more experience with kids—no offense."

"None taken. Well, I'm gonna head on home. Call me as soon as you can." He leaned in and kissed me. "Remember, I love you, and I'm here for you."

I smiled. "I know, and thank you."

Only a few minutes after Quincy left, Gwin arrived. I handed Ruby to her and grabbed my purse.

"So Victor's been in the hospital this whole time?" she asked as I grabbed my car keys from the hook beside the front door.

"Yeah, evidently he was robbed and beaten pretty badly the same night he left me. There was no wallet or ID on him, and he was unconscious for a week. When he woke up, he had no idea who he was."

"Wow, that must've been some beating he took."

I nodded. "Yeah, they said his skull was basically bashed in. He's lucky to even be alive."

"And you're going to see him?"

"Yeah, I spoke with his doctor, and he hopes that maybe seeing me will help jog his memory. He still has no idea who he is, and plus, I need to see him to be sure it's actually Victor they're talking about." I hugged her. "Thanks so much for watching Ruby."

"You know it's no problem. Just be careful, Alex."

I smiled. "You and Q worry too much. I'm going to a hospital, Gwin. There's no safer place for a woman in my condition."

"You know what I mean. I'm not talking about the baby. I'm talking about *you*. You and Quincy are finally getting things back together. Don't risk messing that up for Victor."

I frowned. "What are you talking about? Nothing's changed. Victor and I are over, but I can't just let him sit in that hospital alone and confused. If I can help him with his memory, then I want to do that."

She sighed. "Okay. See you in a little bit."

"Okay," I said as I walked out of the front door. "Thanks, again."

***

I met Dr. Bill Hoffman, a huge, imposing man, in a small room within the Neurology Unit at Methodist Hospital, and when he laid a picture of a badly bruised and battered man before me, I gasped. My hand shot to my mouth. Both of his eyes were blackened, and his face was so swollen; it looked lumpy and distorted.

"That… that's him. That's Victor," I managed to say.

"This is how he presented to our ER. He was badly beaten and bludgeoned with a blunt object—possibly a bat. His skull was fractured, and we had to relieve pressure on his brain. His left leg and right arm were broken. He was found in the middle of a street, unconscious and with no identification. He remained in a coma for a week before awakening with no recollection of who or where he was."

I shook my head. "I didn't even know amnesia was real. I thought it was something you only see in movies."

"With a head injury like your husband's, amnesia can be *very* real."

"How is he now? How is he healing?"

"Physically, he has greatly improved. He's on crutches, but he can walk, and he can take care of his basic needs. Cognitively, he can speak both English and Portuguese fluently, but he has no idea who he is or that he's married with a child on the way. That's where you come in, Mrs. Castro."

I placed my hand on my oversized belly and adjusted in the uncomfortable chair. "You really think I can help him with his memory?"

"Well, there's a theory that in some cases of retrograde amnesia, all it takes is for the patient to see something or someone that is familiar to them in order for them to recover their memory. Up until this point, we didn't know what that could be. I'm hoping that seeing you, a loved one, will help him. I figure it's at least worth a try."

I dropped my eyes, too ashamed to tell him the truth—that I was nothing near a loved one. "Um, okay. Where is he?"

"He's in his room. I can take you there now if you're ready, but I need to be blunt with you. This might not work. It might take years for him to fully recover his memory, and when it happens, it's usually spontaneous."

I sighed. "I see."

"Are you ready to see him?"

I nodded, stood from the chair, and followed him through the unit to Victor's room. I followed him inside and was so shocked at the sight before me, I was left with no words to say.

Victor was sitting on the side of the bed wearing a t-shirt and a pair of scrub bottoms. He'd lost weight, and his head had been shaved. What was left was jagged stubble highlighted by a stitched wound on the right side of his head. His face was scruffy, his jaw was still a little swollen, and there was a heartbreakingly frightened look in his eyes. But despite all of that, Victor was still handsome enough to stop traffic. I was sure the nurses had enjoyed caring for him.

"I've brought someone to see you," Dr. Hoffman said. "Do you recognize her?"

Victor looked up at me, studied me for a while, and then shook his head. "No."

Dr. Hoffman nodded and with a sigh said, "Well, this is your wife."

With a furrowed brow, Victor said, "Wife?"

I nodded. "Yes."

Silence from Victor.

Dr. Hoffman walked to the door. "Well, I'll let you two talk. Hopefully something will be said to jog your memory."

After Dr. Hoffman shut the door behind him, I took a seat in a chair and said, "You don't remember anything at all?"

He stood from the bed on his good leg, grabbed his crutches, and hobbled over to the window, focusing on the scenery outside. "I remember Brazil."

I smiled. "Rio?"

He turned and looked at me. "No. São Paulo."

"You remember São Paulo? That's where you grew up. Do you remember your name?"

"No."

"It's Victor. Victor Castro."

"Victor Castro." He moved closer to me. "Are you really my wife?"

I nodded. "Yes, I'm Alexandria."

"And we are having a baby?"

"Yep, and we already have a daughter." I pulled up a picture on my cell phone and showed it to him. "Ruby."

He held the phone and stared at the picture. "My daughter? She is beautiful."

I smiled again. "She looks a lot like you."

"How old is she?"

"Almost one."

"When is the new baby due?"

"In a few days."

He smiled for the first time since I entered the room. "How long have we been married?"

I dropped my eyes. I felt like this was a test or something. In the back of my mind, I wondered if I should tell him the whole truth about us. Then I decided the time wasn't right. "Almost two years."

"Two years, two babies. We must really love each other," he said, his eyes glued to me.

I was saved from having to respond to him by a light knock at the door. A tall, blonde nurse let herself in. "Sorry to interrupt."

"Candace! Come in, and meet my wife," Victor said warmly. "And guess what? I know my name now. Victor." Even in a hospital with amnesia and a broken arm and leg, Victor oozed charm.

Candace smiled. "It suits you." She walked over to me and handed me a stack of papers. "These are his discharge papers. I'll need you to sign for his release, and then you can take him home. But we sure will miss him. He's been my favorite patient."

I looked from the papers to Victor to the nurse. "Um, discharge? The doctor didn't say anything about him being discharged."

"Well, he actually could've been discharged a few days ago. We were just trying to find somewhere to send him. But since you're here and you're his wife, he can go home with you."

She made it sound so simple, but she had no idea how complicated this was. "Um, can I speak to you outside for a moment?" I asked.

She gave me a quizzical look. "Um... sure."

I glanced over at Victor. "Uh, be right back."

He gave me a little smile in return.

We stepped outside the room, and I closed the door behind us. "Um, look. I can't take him home with me."

Her eyes widened. "What? Are you not his wife?"

"Yes, but things are... are complicated. We weren't getting along very well before all of this happened. We were separating."

"Well, he doesn't remember any of that. And from what I can tell, he's a good guy. Maybe you two can work things out."

"I... I don't think so," I said barely above a whisper.

She sighed. "Look, the only place they could find to send him is a halfway house across town. He's your husband. Surely you'd rather take him home than let him stay in a strange place with convicts and drug addicts."

I looked at the door. No matter what had transpired between us, Victor didn't deserve to be in a place like that. "Okay, maybe it'll be okay... just until he gets on his feet."

She smiled brightly. "Great!"

22

When I entered my home with Victor in tow, Gwin met me at the door with a *what-the-hell-is-going-on* look on her face. Before she could utter a word, I took Ruby from her and said, "Thanks so much, Gwin. Let me get Victor settled, and then I'll walk you out."

I led him into the living room and handed him the remote control. "I'll be right back."

He smiled up at me. "Okay."

I rushed back into the foyer and led Gwin outside. No sooner than the front door swung shut behind us, she said, "Um… Alex, what's going on?"

"They were discharging him, and he had nowhere else to go, Gwin. What was I supposed to do?"

"Put him on a plane back to Brazil where he belongs."

"With a broken arm and a broken leg and amnesia? Come on. That would just be heartless."

"Alex, the man pulled disappearing acts and cheated on you *after* he signed a contract to treat you right! You don't owe him any loyalty."

"It's not about loyalty. I mean, I just figured he should at least be around when I have this baby."

She shook her head. "What are you going to tell Quincy?"

I frowned a little. "You act like Q is my husband and I've moved some other man into our house. *Victor* is still my husband, Gwin."

"*Hired* husband."

"He doesn't know that. He thinks we're in love and making babies like rabbits."

"Then tell him the truth."

"I will, but I don't want to lay too much on him at once. He's been through a lot."

"Mm-hmm. I sure hope you know what you're doing."

"I do."

With raised eyebrows, she said, "Where have I heard that before?"

"That's a cheap shot. Besides, this is different. I'm actually trying to do the right thing."

"So the right thing is to bring a crippled gigolo into your home days before you're due to have your second child. Never mind the fact that you already have a one-year-old to care for."

"It's the right thing if the crippled gigolo is the father of said children."

She unlocked her car door and slid inside. "I swear. I don't know what I'm going to do with you."

I smiled. "You know you love the soap opera that is my life."

"Oh, it's a soap opera, all right. Exotic locations, gigolos, amnesia. All you need is for your long-lost twin sister by a different mother to show up and try to steal your identity."

"I didn't already tell you about her?" I said.

Gwin eyed me, and I laughed. She rolled her eyes and backed out of my driveway.

When I walked back into the house, Victor was standing at the window next to the front door. "Your friend looks upset."

I shrugged. "She's okay. Um, are you hungry or thirsty? Or if you're tired, you can lie down for a while. Are you hurting? You need some pain medication?"

He shook his head. "Can I hold her?"

I nodded and handed Ruby to him. He pulled her to him and hugged her with his good arm and she rested her head on his chest. He closed his eyes and rubbed his hand up and down her little back.

"Do you remember her?" I asked softly.

There were tears in his eyes when he looked up at me and shook his head. "No, but I feel love for her. I feel she's very precious to me. She's in my heart. *She's in my heart.*"

I blinked back my own tears as I watched him hobble into the living room and sit down with her. He didn't let her out of his sight from that moment on. At bedtime, he sat in the rocking chair in her room and rocked her to sleep. Then we both stood by the crib and watched her sleep for a while.

I looked at him, at the peacefulness in his eyes as he watched her, and it warmed my heart. "Um, if you're ready for bed, I can show you to the guest room."

He looked over at me. "Do we not sleep together?"

I folded my arms around my own body. "Um... well... yes, but I didn't think you'd want to sleep with me since you don't remember me… or do you? Do you remember me now?"

He stared at me for a moment, shook his head, and dropped his eyes. "No. I'm sorry."

For some reason, I felt a little relieved that he didn't remember me. "Um, that's okay. Let me show you to your room."

As I turned to leave, he said, "I think it will help if things are as they were before. Maybe if I sleep with you, it will help me remember."

I hesitated, my mind somewhere in between wanting him and not wanting him. "O… okay."

As soon as I agreed, I felt guilty. Hadn't I promised Quincy to start over with him? I'd been dodging his phone calls ever since I brought Victor home that evening, because I honestly didn't know what to say to him, and I was sure he wouldn't understand what I was doing.

I led Victor into our bedroom and pointed to the far side of the bed. "Your side is over there."

He nodded and a small smile inched across his lips. "Is this where we made Ruby?"

I felt my face heat up. "What? Uh… no, we made her in São Paulo, during our honeymoon. Um, I'm gonna take a shower. There's another bathroom down the hall if you need to take one. Towels are on the shelf in there. You have a few clothes in the dresser, some underwear and stuff."

Nearly an hour later, I emerged from the steamy bathroom and walked into my dark bedroom. I could see Victor's body beneath the covers on his side of the bed. I took a deep breath and told myself that I could do this. He was my husband, after all, and I'd slept with him before. Plus, all we were going to do was sleep. Shoot, I was too pregnant to do anything more than that.

No sooner than I slipped into bed, I felt Victor scoot close to me and rest his arm on my expanded waist. "Is this how I held you?" he whispered in my ear.

I jumped up and turned the lamp on. "What... what are you doing?"

He gave me a confused look. "Trying to remember."

"Well, you can't just grab me like that without warning."

"Sorry. I thought it would be okay to hold you. I thought maybe you missed me. After all, we're in love, yeah?"

I sighed. "It's okay. It's just that with the baby coming, I need my space."

"Oh, I understand. I won't bother you again, querida."

"What did you call me?"

"Querida?"

"You used to call me that a lot. Remember?"

He shrugged. "It just came out, but maybe I *am* remembering. Maybe being here with you is working."

I nodded. "Good. Okay, well, goodnight then."

"Goodnight."

He rolled over in the bed, and I reclaimed my spot and turned the lamp off. I lay there for a few minutes before turning over to face his back. "How... how does it feel?" I asked.

"How does what feel?" he said softly.

"Not being able to remember. How does that feel?"

I felt him roll over. "It feels like… like a bad dream, a nightmare that will not end. In the hospital, I tried so hard to remember who I was, what I was. Was I good or bad? Had I hurt anyone? Did anyone miss me? Did anyone… love me? I was afraid to know, afraid not to know. It was… it was *torture*. I began to wonder if I was real or not. I… I wasn't sure. But now there's you and Ruby. So I know."

"You know what?"

"I know that I am real, that I am loved. It's not so bad now. It's better."

I didn't know what to say. So I just said, "Um… good. Well, goodnight, again." Then I rolled over and closed my eyes.

"Goodnight," he whispered as I drifted off to sleep.

23

"Get It Together"

The sun had barely risen the next morning when I heard the doorbell ring. I looked over at Victor's side of the bed and found it empty. I climbed out of bed, grabbed my robe, which barely wrapped around my belly, and threw it on. I walked down the hall to Ruby's room to find her crib empty. Figuring Victor had her, I headed downstairs to answer the door. When I reached the foyer, my stomach dropped. Standing in the doorway was Victor with Ruby in one arm and a crutch under the other. And standing outside was Quincy with a look on his face that was somewhere in between shock and anger.

I rushed to the door. "I've got it, Victor," I said, pushing past him.

He shrugged. "Okay." He smiled and retreated into the house.

I walked outside and closed the door. "Q, what are you doing here so early?"

He frowned. "I was worried. I called you all day yesterday, and you never answered. I thought maybe something happened with the baby. I tried talking to Gwin, but she was saying all these weird, cryptic things. So I decided to come check for myself. What is going on, Alex? Why is he here?"

"They were going to send him to a halfway house, and I just didn't feel like it was right to let that happen."

"Why not?!" he asked, raising his voice. "He's nothing to you! He's just the hired help. You don't owe him anything!"

"He is Ruby's father, and he's far from his home and his family. I'm all he has right now. And it's just until he's back on his feet. Until he gets his memory back."

"Until—how long is that supposed to take?!"

"Q, can you lower your voice, please?"

"Lower my voice? Are you for real, Alex? You let him back into your life? You're letting him be around Ruby?"

"Have you forgotten that he is her father, Q?" I asked with widened eyes.

"I'm more of a father to her than he is!"

"What? You've spent a couple of weeks with her. Come on, you are really overreacting, here."

"Overreacting? You're supposed to divorce him, Alex. How you gon' do that with him all up in your house?! What are you doing? What about us?"

I stepped closer to him. "Nothing has changed, Q. I just want to help him. I owe him that much as the father of my babies. Will you just try to understand that?"

"I don't believe it."

"You don't believe what?"

"I don't believe he has no amnesia. He's faking it."

I sighed. "Why in the world would he be faking it, Q?"

"So that you'll feel sorry for him and give him another chance. I'd do the same thing if I was him. No lie, I would."

I shook my head. "He can't fake getting his skull smashed. I saw the pictures, talked to the doctor. He's not faking it."

"I still don't think it's your duty to help him."

"Well, *I* think it is."

He shook his head. "I don't know about this."

"Look, I'm willing to give you a chance despite what you did with Farrah. Why can't you understand that I need to help him?"

"You got to bring that up?"

"It's the truth. If you want mercy from me, you've got to let me show him some mercy, too. I'm just going to help him get on his feet. Then I'll divorce him, and we can move on, okay?"

He placed his hands on my arms. "Just be careful."

"I'm going to be fine. Victor is harmless. He just needs my support right now."

He kissed my cheek. "All right, I guess. Call me later?"

"Sure."

I released a relieved sigh as I watched him climb back into his car and pull out of my driveway.

I returned to my house to find Victor and Ruby in the kitchen. Ruby was in her highchair, and Victor was at the stove, cooking.

"You remember how to cook, huh?" I asked as I took a seat at the table.

Without looking up he said, "I remember many things." He turned around and looked at me. "But I do not remember that man. Who was he?"

"He is my ex-fiancé."

"He seemed angry to see me here."

"No, I think he was just surprised. You were gone for weeks."

"I was in the hospital."

"I know."

"Are you having an affair with him?" he asked as he walked over to the table.

"Where are your crutches? You really should use them. I don't think you should be walking on that cast. And how in the world did you make it down the stairs with Ruby all by yourself?"

He adjusted his arm in the sling as he sat down across from me. "Are you having an affair with him?" he repeated.

"No, I'm not."

"How were we before I was hurt?"

"What do you mean?"

"How were we? Were we good together?"

I clasped my hands on the table and fixed my eyes on them. "Sometimes."

"Sometimes?"

"Our relationship was… complicated."

"But you love me?"

I hesitated, wanted to lie, but couldn't. "Yes."

"And I loved you?"

"I don't know."

"I think I did, or I do."

I looked up at him. "Why do you say that?"

"Because a baby as beautiful and peaceful as Ruby could only be created in love."

I smiled a little as I looked over at her. "Really?"

"Really."

We were silent for a few moments as the kitchen began to fill with the scent of whatever Victor was cooking.

"What's for breakfast?" I asked.

"Toast, eggs, and fruit. I think you like that, yeah?"

I nodded and smiled again—a little wider this time. "I do."

"Good."

"Hey, would you like to speak to your mother? I know you don't remember her, but she's been very worried about you, and it might help you to talk to her. And I promised her I'd have you call her."

He nodded enthusiastically. "Sure."

I dialed her number on my cell phone and activated the speakerphone. She answered after the first ring.

"Mrs. Castro? It's Alexandria."

"Yes, yes. I got your message about Victor! Is he there with you now?"

"Yes, ma'am."

"Victor?" she said.

Victor's expression changed. I could see the recognition in his eyes, followed by a stream of tears. He rested his elbows on the table, held his head in his hands, and began to blurt out a fluid stream of Portuguese. The next thing I knew, the two of them were having an entire conversation in this language that I didn't understand. I wondered what they were talking about. Did he remember me, now?

After he and his mother ended their phone call, Victor hobbled over to the stove, cut it off, and went into the living room where he sat on the sofa and stared into space. I picked up Ruby, and with her on my hip, I followed him. I sat down next to him, but he didn't turn his head or acknowledge my presence in any way.

"You remember your mother?" I asked, then felt stupid for asking. It was obvious he remembered her.

He glanced over at me, took Ruby from my arms, and nodded. "Yes."

"What else do you remember?"

He sighed. "I remember growing up in São Paulo. I remember my brothers and sister. I remember being poor and hungry. I remember how my mother would work so hard to take care of us. And I remember my father…"

"Your father? I didn't get a chance to meet him. As a matter of fact, I don't remember you even mentioning him before."

He closed his eyes and rested against the back of the sofa, hugging Ruby tightly to him. "I am sure I did not want to talk about him."

"Oh, I see. I'm not very close to my father, either."

No reply from Victor.

"What did you and your mother talk about? I don't speak

Portuguese."

"I did not think you did," he said, not really answering my question.

I sat there for a few moments before realizing that he didn't want to talk. Something he had remembered or something that was said between him and his mother had dampened his mood, and he was quiet for the rest of the day. It wasn't until we'd settled into bed that night that he spoke again. With my back to him, I heard him speak in a small voice.

"I do not talk about my father, because I do not like him," he said.

I stared into the darkness. "Well, we're more alike than I realized. I don't like mine, either. He left when I was young, and he never looked back."

"At least your father left. He did not stay and torture you." His voice quivered as he spoke those last words.

I turned to face him, though I couldn't see him in the darkness. "Do you... do you want to tell me what happened?"

I heard him sniffle. "You're my wife. I guess I can tell you if no one else."

I felt a pang of guilt but knew this wasn't the time to explain the complications of our marriage. "If you want to," I said softly, "I'll listen."

He released a long, ragged sigh. "He was a very mean man. He would... he would drink a lot, and the liquor made him very mean to all of us children but never my mother. He never hurt her."

"Why was he mean to the kids?" I asked.

"I always thought it was because there were so many of us. Eight in all. I think he felt that he could not take care of us, and it frustrated him. He was a laborer. My mother was a maid. There was never enough food. Not enough clothes. I think he saw us as burdens."

"And your mother? She… she knew he was mean to you all?"

"Yes, she knew. He would beat us with belts or his hands, and she would never say a word. She did not want to disrespect him. She never tried to stop him or help us. When I was young, I hated her, too."

"But you don't hate her now. You two are, or were, close."

"After my father died, we grew closer. I realized she was weak… I needed her, so I forgave her."

"How did your father die?"

He laughed bitterly. "He was found dead in his car. He was naked. He had been shot. I wish he had suffered more."

I wasn't sure what to say in response, so I didn't say anything.

"The police told my mother that a prostitute shot him, because he tried to rape her."

"Victor…"

He ignored me and continued to speak. "I remember thinking that prostitute was a hero, that she had freed all of us from him. From the beatings and the screaming. From his hatred."

I closed my eyes and thought about what he'd just said. Suddenly a lot of things about him made sense to me, and after almost two years of marriage, I felt like I was finally, really getting to know him.

"It surprises me that I have a wife and children," he said.

"W… why?"

"Because I remember saying I would never get married and have children. I was always so afraid I would end up like my father. I was afraid it was in my blood."

I reached over in the darkness and found his face, rested my hand on his cheek. "You're nothing like him, Victor."

"Are you sure? I… I cannot remember how things were between us before. If I ever hurt you—"

I placed a finger to his lips. "You didn't," I lied. But was it really a lie? He hadn't done anything remotely like what he'd described his father doing, but he *had* hurt me, or had I hurt myself by falling for him? After all, I knew our arrangement from the beginning. Falling in love was not planned. How could I blame him for how I felt?

"Good. I know you're special, and I must love you very much."

"Why do you say that?"

"Because I married you. I do not think I would have done that unless I loved you very deeply."

"But you still can't remember me."

"I know, and it troubles me."

"Well, your memories are coming back to you pretty rapidly. So maybe you'll remember me soon."

"I know I will remember nothing but love. I can feel it from you, you know? I feel your love in the way you care for Ruby. I see it in your eyes when you look at me." He reached over and rested his hand on my face. Then he inched closer and gently kissed my lips. I closed my eyes and received his kiss. I wrapped my arms around him as he pulled my body to his. We kissed for a long while as a mutual passion burned inside of each of us, and at that moment, I forgot about our past or the terms of our life together. At that moment, I felt him like I never had before. I felt nothing but true love from him and for him.

"See, I can feel it," he said once our lips had parted.

Two days later, exactly one day prior to my due date, I went into labor. Since Victor was still sporting two casts and a sling, Gwin came and picked all of us up and dropped Ruby off at my mother's house. My mother, who knew about me and Quincy and of course preferred him to Victor, gave me *the eye* when she came out to the car to see me off and wish me good luck.

Gwin was quiet on the way to the hospital, but then again, I already knew how she felt about the situation. What was I supposed to do, though? Ban Victor from the hospital for doing some stuff he didn't even remember doing? How would that have been right? Plus, he was my husband and the father of the child I was about to deliver. If anyone should've been there, it was him.

Thankfully, we made it to the hospital in no time, and I was rushed back to Labor and Delivery where I didn't have to deal with Gwin's judgment or Victor's confusion. Until they were allowed into the room, I could clear my mind and breathe and forget about the melodrama that was my life. After they hooked me up to the monitors and I was able to hear the galloping heartbeat of my baby, my mind began to clear, and I knew that everything was worth what I'd been through. The contractions came faster and faster, as did the labor process as a whole. Things sped along quicker than they had with Ruby, and soon, Victor and Gwin were both in the room coaching me through the delivery.

Victor was present when Ruby was born, and he was very supportive, but something was different this time. There was this wonder and awe in his eyes. He behaved and looked like a child visiting Disneyland for the first time. And when the doctor pulled our baby from my body and lifted her up for us to see, Victor clutched his chest and began crying. He kissed my forehead and thanked me profusely, and in that moment, I knew this was not the same man I'd married. I knew he was different. Not just "lost memory" different, but something in his spirit and his heart had changed. It was almost as if by losing his memory, he had shed a darker part of himself, leaving space for a lighter, purer part of himself to break forth.

I smiled at him as he cut the umbilical cord. And when the nurse brought our baby to me and laid her on my chest, I smiled, laughed a little, and said, "Another girl. She's so beautiful."

Victor nodded in agreement. "Just like her mother."

I rubbed my finger across her little forehead and thanked God that she was perfect in every way.

***

Victor spent the night in my room. Actually, Victor never left my side from the time they allowed him into the labor room until the day we returned home with both of our daughters. We decided to name our newest daughter Daisy, after Victor's mother. And there we were in our home—a family of four. It felt good, so good that I forgot all about Quincy. Well, that is until he showed up at my front door.

Victor answered the doorbell, and when I heard him call my name, I hesitated for a moment. Something told me that it was Quincy. I slowly walked to the door with Daisy in my arms and found that my suspicions were correct. Standing there with a strained look on his face and a pink gift bag in his hand was Quincy. Victor was leaning on his crutches, watching me walk into the foyer.

I looked up at Victor and said, "Thanks, I've got it."

Victor nodded and leaned in to kiss me. Out of the corner of my eye, I could see Quincy glaring at him. Once I was sure Victor was out of earshot, I said, "Hey, I wasn't expecting you."

He shook his head and shrugged. "Yeah, well, I wasn't expecting you and your hired husband to be so cozy up in here, either. So this is how things are, Alex? You playing house with him again?"

I sighed. "What I'm trying to figure out is what is so bad about me living and raising my children with my husband. *Husband*, Q. Not some random stranger off the street. I am married to the man!"

"A husband who is a hired-damn-gigolo, or did you forget? Is amnesia contagious or something?"

I dropped my eyes. "No, I didn't forget."

"Oh, okay, then you remember all those late nights he was out with other women, and you remember how he disappeared for a week when you were still pregnant, right?"

"Yes, but—"

"And just because he can't remember any of that stuff, he gets a 'get out of jail free card?!' How does that make sense? He doesn't love you, Alex. He's using you. You are his paycheck. I don't care if he can't remember it, *he is using you.*"

"What about the fact that I love him?"

"You don't love him. You love this fantasy you've got in your head. You love this whole 'married with children' fairy tale."

"I'm not some little girl, Q. I know what love is, and I know how I feel about him."

He frowned. "Wait… are you backing out on me?"

"Backing out of what?"

"*Us.* You've changed your mind?"

"Look, I know what we discussed about the future, but I never promised you anything."

"Huh," he scoffed. "You said you were going to divorce him and give us another try. You said him being here wouldn't change anything, but clearly, it has. Now you've got a selective-damn-memory."

I shook my head. "No, but things are different and Victor is different and we're happy."

"You're *happy*? You're happy because he can't *remember* to dog you out! What are you going to do when he does?"

"I don't know."

He closed his eyes. Seconds later, they popped open. "Is this about the thing with Farrah? You're still holding that against me? I thought you were over that."

I adjusted my baby in my arms. "Over it? Q, I'll never be *over it.* I forgive you, and I choose not to dwell on it. But over it? How could I be *over* you having sex with my sister?"

"Look, I told you I'm sorry. But how is what I did with Farrah any different from what he did with whomever he did it with?"

"For one, he didn't have sex with anyone who shares my DNA."

"How do you know that? Farrah's scandalous, and you said she's always drooling over him. And he's a ho', so if the price was right, he just might have hooked up with her."

I shook my head. "You don't know that to be true. You're just grasping at straws. *Plus*, Farrah's broke. She couldn't *afford* Victor."

"You don't know it to be false. Maybe he did it for free. He's a gigolo. I'm sure he likes sex. You better think about what you're doing, and remember who that man really is. You're trying to live some fairy tale with that dude in there. *I'm* your reality, Alex. I'm willing to be with you, marry you, and raise those girls, and I'm willing to wait. But I won't wait forever."

He handed me the gift bag and then he left, leaving behind troubling thoughts that wouldn't vacate my mind.

24

"Gettin' In the Way"

Daisy was a week old before my family converged on my house. Of course, my mother had visited her in the hospital. But on this day, at my house, she brought along a host of cousins, aunts, uncles, my niece and nephew… and Farrah. She must've been hiding behind someone or something, because I didn't even notice her until everyone was in the living room crowded around Victor, who held Daisy proudly in his arms.

"Everyone, you already know Victor. Victor, this is my family. I don't know if you remember anyone?" I said.

Victor just smiled and shrugged. I think he was so proud to be showing the baby off, it didn't matter to him that he was in a room full of strangers. Mama swiped Daisy from his arms and moved over to the loveseat. The crowd followed her like a swarm of bees following the queen bee. I sat down next to Victor who quickly grasped my hand. And Farrah sat down next to me, much to my dismay.

"So, how you been? Two babies in two years. I think you outdid me," she said with a stupid grin on her face.

"I'm fine," I said flatly.

She leaned forward and fixed her eyes on Victor. "How are *you*, Victor."

I took my hand, placed it on her chest, and pushed her back against the sofa. "He's fine, too."

She threw her hair over her shoulder and gave me an impish grin. "Humph, I can see *that*."

I sat there, speechless. Not because of what she said, but because of the aroma that wafted from her neck when she tossed her hair. She was wearing perfume, but not just any perfume. It was the same perfume I had smelled on Victor after one of his late night engagements. I could never forget that scent. It was the same perfume. I *knew* it was.

My stomach began to churn. Quincy was right. Victor had slept with Farrah. Farrah had slept with my husband. *My husband*. Was there nothing she wouldn't do to hurt me? As I sat there and let the revelation soak into my mind, the room began to spin around me and my heart began to thunder in my chest and my ears. My breathing grew louder, and then everything went silent. It was as if someone had pressed a mute button and all of the benign chatter and other noises surrounding me had ceased. I looked around the room at the smiling faces, at my mother as her lips moved, at one of my cousins who was talking to Victor, at Farrah whose mouth was flapping like a fish's tailfin. Surely I hadn't gone deaf. But what else could explain the sudden absence of sound?

"So y'all gonna have some more?" Farrah said as my hearing returned.

I glared at her and almost involuntarily, I screamed, "Get out!"

Everyone and everything in the room stopped, and all eyes were on me.

"Could everyone please leave now?" I said in a much calmer voice. "Especially you, Farrah. I want you to get out of here and never come back, you hear me? I don't even want to see you drive that raggedy car of yours down my street again. If you do, there's gonna be hell to pay!"

"Farrah, what'd you do?" Mama asked as she struggled to her feet while holding my baby.

Farrah wore a rather convincingly shocked expression. "Nothing! She's gone crazy. All I said was that Victor is fine. Shoot, Helen Keller, Stevie Wonder, *and* Ray Charles can see that. I didn't say nothing that wasn't true."

"Well, you don't have no business talking about her husband like that," Mama said as she walked over to the sofa and handed the baby back to Victor, who looked so confused I almost felt sorry for him. "Come on, y'all. Let's go. I know Alex is probably tired, and it's too many of us up in here at one time," Mama added.

Mama reached for me and gave me a tight hug. "Call me if you need some help," she whispered in my ear.

One by one, my family members filed out of my house with Farrah bringing up the rear.

"You really should think about seeing a therapist or something. Those mood swings can't be safe for the kids *or* Victor," Farrah said as she walked out the door.

I don't know what made me snap. Maybe it was the little smirk she wore, or the way she said Victor's name. Or maybe it was the fact that I never kicked her tail for sleeping with Quincy. But I think the real reason I ran up behind her, snatched her up by her hair, and punched her in the mouth was that she'd slept with my husband, the man I loved. And when the images of her in bed with him, touching him and enjoying him, flooded my mind, I found myself unable to stop hitting her.

I pummeled my sister for what felt like ages, and despite the fact that my fist and arm hurt, I didn't, or maybe I *couldn't,* stop. I needed to punish her.

I needed to hurt her the way she'd hurt me.

The shouts from my mother didn't stop me. My cousins couldn't pull me off of her. Victor's shocked face didn't deter me. The only thing that made me snap back into reality was the sight of a police cruiser pulling to a stop at the edge of my driveway with its blue and red lights flashing. In the commotion, which had started inside my house and spilled out into the driveway, I guess a neighbor had called the police, and I suddenly had the presence of mind to realize I could be arrested for what I was doing, so I stopped hitting her, stood to my feet, and watched as she stumbled to hers.

She grabbed her pretty, bloody face and shouted, "You are crazy! *Insane!*"

I smiled a little and softly said, "I know."

The police came, took one look at me and Farrah, and arrested both of us despite the protests of my relatives. As they walked me out to the car, I looked back at Victor, who was holding Daisy in his arms, and I began to cry.

***

I was only in jail a few hours before Victor bailed me out. As he walked me out to the car, I noticed the crutches were missing, as was the cast on his leg.

"Where's your cast?" I asked.

"It was getting in the way."

"You took it off yourself?"

"Yes," he said as he pulled the car onto the street.

"How?"

"With a saw."

"Oh." I peered out the side window. "I guess my mom bailed Farrah out."

"I have no idea."

"Where are the babies?"

"With your friend, Gwin. Your mother sent her over. She knew I would need the help."

"I'm sorry, Victor. I know I put you in a bad situation with your injuries and everything."

Silence from Victor.

When we finally made it home, Victor exited the car without uttering a single word to me. I just sat there, not wanting to go inside to face Gwin or my own mess of a life. I sat there for about ten minutes before Gwin emerged from the house with Ruby on her hip.

She snatched the door open. "Get your crazy ass out of that car!"

I climbed out of the car. "You don't have to yell."

"Evidently, I do. How you gonna get yourself arrested like that? You have two babies, Alex. *Two*. Poor Victor was lost when I got here. How could you do something like this? Was Farrah really worth all that?! I mean, if you are still mad about the whole Quincy thing then something is seriously wrong with you. Girl, that's ancient history, and I thought you were so happy with Victor now. What in the world got into you?"

I hung my head. "I found out she slept with Victor."

"What? Who? Farrah?"

"Yes."

"She told you that?"

"No, it was her perfume. It was the same perfume I smelled on Victor before."

"So, you are basing this on some perfume? Alex, are you serious? If Farrah was wearing that perfume, you know it was cheap. The girl has no taste *or* money. Shoot, half of the hood-rat population of Houston probably wears that perfume."

I shook my head. "No, it was her. She's been drooling over Victor since the day she laid eyes on him. And she hates me. She'd do anything to make my life miserable."

"Okay, none of that is evidence of her guilt. She's always hated you, and drooling over Victor means nothing. Honey, I just finished drooling over him, myself. The man is fine, Alex. *Ridiculously* fine."

I sighed. "I just believe it was her."

"Well, did Victor confirm it?"

"Come on now, Gwin. He doesn't even remember me and Ruby. He's not going to remember sleeping with Farrah."

Gwin handed Ruby to me. "Maybe it's time for you to jog his memory."

"What do you mean by that?"

"Tell him about your marriage and how you met. Get it all out in the open. And ask him about Farrah, too."

"I don't know. Things between us are good. I love him, Gwin. I can't deny that anymore. I love him, and I would love to spend my life with him."

"So it's over for you and Quincy?"

"It's *been* over for us. I was just trying to get Victor out of my heart, but I couldn't. What I felt for Quincy is nothing in comparison to what I feel for Victor."

"And you're afraid that if Victor remembers the truth, he'll leave?"

"Yeah. Once he remembers he signed a contract and that all the terms have been met, I'm *sure* he'll want a divorce. And if he remembers me beating him up, I'm more than sure he'll wanna leave. And… and what if he's in love with Farrah?"

"Alex…"

"I think that's what made me so angry. That's why I hit her. I couldn't stand the thought of him loving her."

Gwin rested her hand on my shoulder. "Alex, sweetie, I don't think he loves her. And let me say this: you know you're my girl and I love you, but you're gonna have to do something about your temper. You're gonna get in a real mess one day, and you don't need that. Your babies need you."

I nodded. "I know. I'll think about what you've said."

"While you're thinking, think about this: Victor is going to remember one day, and when he does, he's going to wonder why you didn't just tell him the truth. The way I see it, you stand a chance of losing him either way, but maybe if you're honest, he'll take that into consideration. You know, I think I was right about him the first time. I spent a little time with him before he left to bail you out. He was so worried. He seems to really care about you and the girls."

"That's the thing, Gwin. It's like you said before. I think he's always loved me. I think he was just afraid to show it before. When he lost his memory, he was able to let his guard down."

"Yeah. Look, I gotta go before *my* husband leaves *me*. Talk to you later."

"Okay."

I walked into my house to find Victor in the living room with both of the babies—Ruby in his arms, Daisy asleep in her bassinette. I sat down on the couch next to him and sighed.

"Why do you hate your sister?" he asked before my butt hit the cushion good.

I shrugged. "It's a long story."

"Tell me."

I looked over at him and sighed again. "She's hated me since we were kids. I've never understood why. But she's always hated me. Always took things from me. She… she had sex with Quincy when we were engaged. And she…"

"What?"

"I don't know. I guess I just got tired of her and her smart remarks."

"And the way she looks at me?"

I nodded. "You noticed that?"

"Yes, but I do not want her."

"You want me?"

"Yes. Very much."

I smiled a little and shook my head. "But you don't know me. You don't remember me."

"My heart knows you, and it tells me that I love you." He leaned in and kissed me. "And when the doctor says it is good to do so, I will show you I love you with my body."

"I wish you really meant it," I muttered under my breath.

"What?"

"Nothing."

He smiled at me as he gently stroked my cheek. "You are beautiful. Your sister does not compare. Do not worry about her or let her make you angry."

I placed my hand over his. "I'll try not to."

He pulled me close to him, and I rested against his body.

25

I had my day in court and was sentenced to probation and mandatory anger management classes. I guess I needed the classes. I suppose there was something wrong with the fact that I tended to get a little physically violent from time to time, but I happened to believe I had cause for those outbursts. Infidelity and betrayal are bitter pills to swallow, and sometimes enough is just enough.

I attended the classes twice weekly and met some pretty strange people—mostly men. I guess women are usually a little more in control of their anger. I don't know, but it felt strange being in the room with those people and listening to their stories. I mean, I wasn't as bad off as them, was I? You could count the total number of fights I'd had in my entire life on one hand. Well, that's if you didn't count the fights I had as a kid, and you really couldn't count those anyway, could you? At any rate, I didn't think I had any business in that room with those people. But I went, anyway, in order to fulfill the court order and keep myself out of trouble. Victor stayed with the girls while I attended the classes, since only a few days after my arrest, his arm cast was removed. He still didn't remember me, but that was okay, because at least he loved me and he treated me like a wife. If this was the only way I could have a real marriage, I didn't care if he ever really remembered me.

Days passed by and soon, they turned into weeks. When Daisy turned six weeks old, I decided to have both her and Ruby dedicated at my church. When I called my pastor to discuss the dedication with her, I expected her to refuse, since I hadn't been to my own church in forever, but she didn't. Her only stipulation was that she meet with me a couple of weeks prior to the ceremony.

It felt both familiar and strange to walk into my church, a church I had attended since I was a child. As I made my way to Elder Pointer's office, I began to feel a little nervous. After all, I had been avoiding her since I married Victor. But she welcomed me into the pastor's study with a warm smile. She sat down across from me and asked me about myself and my family, and she seemed genuinely interested. Then she ran down the details of the dedication.

"You can invite as many family members as you'd like, and any and all of them can stand with you as witnesses. I'll pray over both girls as you and your husband lay hands on them. The ceremony won't take long, but it is a very powerful occasion. I am so glad you asked me to do this," she said.

"Of course. And thank you for agreeing to do it," I responded. I'd begun to gather my purse to leave when she stopped me in my tracks.

"Alex, is everything okay?" she asked.

I looked at her and nodded. "Yes, like I said, we're fine."

She sighed and reclined in her high-backed chair. With her smooth, ebony skin and crown of salt and pepper braids, she looked regal and beautiful. "How long have I known you, Alexandria?" she asked.

I shrugged. "Since I was a kid, I guess."

"You know, it hurts my feelings that you think you can't come to me."

"I don't... I don't think that..."

"Evidently, you do."

I sighed and locked my eyes on the beige carpet beneath my feet. "I guess I was... I've been ashamed."

"You shouldn't be. I'm here to help, not judge. Now, how have things really been with you?"

I continued to stare at the floor in silence.

"Well, I won't push you. Just know that I am here whenever you want to talk."

I nodded as I slipped my purse strap over my shoulder and stood from the chair. "Thank you."

"You're more than welcome."

I drove home and was greeted by Ruby, who was walking, and sometimes running, all over the place. Victor was right behind her with a chubby little Daisy in his arms. He smiled, kissed me on the cheek, and ushered me into the kitchen where he was preparing my favorite Brazilian meal—Vatapá, a dish made from bread, shrimp, coconut milk, finely ground peanuts and palm oil. I sat at the table and watched as he manned the stove, taking little breaks to play with the girls, or pull me into his arms to dance to imaginary music. He was happy—we were *all* happy. We ate dinner together, put the girls to bed, and then climbed into bed ourselves.

"Eu te amo, eu vou te amar para sempre," he said as he pulled me into his arms.

The words, though I didn't understand them, were so beautiful, they brought me to tears. "What did you say?" I asked softly.

He kissed my eyes and smiled. "I said, 'I love you, I will love you forever.'"

I let my tears flow freely as I rested my hand on his cheek. He was such a beautiful man. "I will love you forever, too."

He gingerly kissed every inch of my brown skin from my forehead to my pinky toe, and then he gently, slowly, tenderly, gave his love to me. Evidently, lovemaking is one of those intrinsic skills that are not affected by memory loss. The only difference I could find in his love making was that it was more passionate, more gentle, and yet, more urgent. When he was finished, he declared his love for me over and over again. And as I lay my head on my pillow, and fell asleep that night, I felt like my prayers had finally been answered.

***

I had been deep in my writing cave that entire day, trying to meet yet another deadline. Victor had graciously agreed to watch the girls so that I could have some peace and quiet to write and think. He'd even brought my breakfast and lunch right into my office to me. I only left that room to use the toilet. When I finally called it quits around six that evening, I emerged from my office, to find my house dark and quiet. I wondered if Victor had left with the girls, and if so, where had they gone?

As I walked past the living room, a flicker of light caught my eye. I slowly entered the room to find it aglow with what must've been hundreds of candles. I stood and took in the scene, and a smile crept upon my lips when a set of hands covered my eyes.

"It is not ready, yet," Victor said.

I reached up and covered his hands with mine. "It's beautiful."

He spun me around to face him and pulled me into a deep kiss. When he released me, he said, "Not as beautiful as you."

"Thank you. Um, are the girls asleep?"

"No, your mother is watching them for us tonight."

"No kids? Wow. What are we going to do?"

"Hmm, use your imagination," he said as he nuzzled my neck.

My heart began to race. "I see."

"Ready for dinner?"

"Yes, I'm starving."

We sat on the living room floor and ate Acarajé and a green salad and washed everything down with my favorite white wine. After we filled our stomachs, Victor turned on the stereo. Soothing ocean sounds filled the room, and when he pulled me into his arms, it almost felt like we were back on my hotel room balcony in Rio.

I lay down on the floor as he kissed my forehead, then my ear, nose, and finally, my lips. He stared at me and smiled. "Come on."

I didn't bother to ask him where we were going, because it didn't matter as long as we were together. I returned his smile and took his hand as he helped me to my feet and led me out onto the patio. "Wait here," he said.

The ocean sounds were replaced by the soothing rhythmic sounds of Brazilian jazz. As the music filled my home and spilled out into my backyard, Victor took me into his arms and began to lead me in a dance. I rested my head on his chest.

"This reminds me of Rio, of when we first met. Do you remember?" I asked.

He tightened his hold on me. "No, querida. I wish I did."

I closed my eyes. "It's okay."

"We can make new memories."

"Yes, we can."

He backed away a little and looked me in the eye. "I do not remember meeting you or falling in love with you or taking vows with you, but I am glad you found me in that hospital. I am glad you brought me home to be with you and my daughters. I am glad you showed me your love, and I am glad I could fall in love with you again. I love you always, querida. *Always.*"

He cupped my face in his hands and kissed me so deeply, I thought I could feel his very soul. "I love you, too, Victor," I whispered once our lips parted. "I love you so much."

He pulled me back into his arms, and we began to sway to the music again. "Your birthday is soon, yeah?"

"You remembered?"

"No, it is circled on the calendar in your office."

"Oh… well, yeah, it is."

"I want to celebrate in Brazil."

"You do?"

"Yes, we can take Ruby and Daisy, and we can see my mother, eat her cooking, see São Paulo, and maybe we can relive some of our memories. Maybe it will help me remember."

"Maybe it will," I said softly.

He kissed me lightly. "We go, then?"

"Sure, I miss Brazil, and your mother needs to see the girls."

"Good!"

We danced a little more. Kissed a little more. Touched and caressed one another, and loved each other until we both fell asleep right there on the patio.

26

"Remember the Time."

I sat in the room full of people and sighed. I could've done without another evening of stupid little anger management tips like "simply walk away," "take deep breaths," and "count to ten." I was fed up to here with learning the symptoms of anger or the effects of anger or the repercussions of unchecked anger. I already knew all of that, and it hadn't kept me from kicking anyone's butt, yet.

I adjusted myself in my chair and wondered what Victor and my girls were doing. I wished I was home with them enjoying some Brazilian cuisine and Brazilian music with my Brazilian husband. I missed my home and my family.

As the class began, I focused my eyes on the facilitator—a petite brunette named, Fran Hinckley—who'd probably never even raised her voice a day in her life.

"Welcome, everyone. I hope you've enjoyed a peaceful few days since our last meeting," she said in her usual bright, sunny voice. Her opening remarks were met with murmurs from a few of the participants.

"Okay, well, we're going to do something a little different this evening. Instead of me talking to you, *you're* going to talk to *me*."

Oh, great, I thought.

She began to hand out sheets of paper and pencils. "The root of anger is usually one of three things: fear, frustration, or pain," she said. "I want each of you to think about your most recent angry outburst and write down what triggered it. Was it fear, frustration, or pain? On the back of that same sheet of paper, think back to the very first time you felt that feeling of fear or pain or frustration which led to intense feelings of anger, and write that down along with how you dealt with those feelings that first time."

I took my sheet of paper and easily completed the first half of the task. My most recent outburst was my altercation with Farrah, and what I was feeling at the time was a combination of fear, pain, *and* frustration. I admittedly feared that Victor loved Farrah and maybe even preferred her to me. I was frustrated with the fact that Farrah had managed to bed the man I loved... *again.* And I was hurt that Victor would betray me in that way, despite the fact that at the time, our marriage was not a real one.

"If you find that all three emotions played a part in your anger, try to choose the one that was most dominant," Fran added, breaking into my thoughts.

In that case, frustration would be my emotion of choice. Frustration was definitely a big problem for me.

On to part two of the assignment. My first feelings of intense anger that resulted from frustration. *This is not going to be easy,* I thought. I'd had problems with my temper for as long as I could remember. I just hadn't always acted on my anger. I sighed as I closed my eyes and thought all the way back to my childhood, to the time before my father left. To an event I hadn't thought about in several years. And the memories and deep feelings of fear and frustration came flooding back to me. I could think of nothing but that time so long ago, a time I had pushed to the back of my mind and filed away. I was so preoccupied with my own thoughts; I didn't hear Fran when she called my name, and when I finally realized she was waiting for me to speak, all I could do was stammer out a few nonsensical words. Thankfully, she moved on to the next person and pulled the spotlight away from me.

I was relieved when the class was over, and was trying to make a quick exit when Fran stopped me in my tracks. "Alex, are you okay?"

I stared at her for a few seconds, almost deciding to tell her the truth, but then decided against it. "No... yes, I'm fine."

"Are you sure?"

"Yes, but I need to get home."

She eyed me skeptically. "Okay... well, see you next week."

"Yes, okay."

I left the building and instead of heading home, drove straight to my mother's house. Mama answered the door in her favorite turquoise housecoat with a pink, silk bonnet on her head. Her signature cat-woman, wire-rimmed glasses were balanced on the end of her wide nose. Looking at her was like looking at an older version of myself—the same peachy, brown skin, the same nose and thick lips. Looking at Mama made me understand what Quincy and Victor saw in me. Mama was beautiful.

"What's goin' on, Alex? What you doing here so late?"

I checked my watch. It was a little past 8:00 PM, but I guess it was late for her. "I'm sorry. Were you in bed?"

She shook her head as she led me into the living room. "Naw, I was just watching a Lifetime movie. Got to give Wesley his nine o'clock pills before I can go to bed." She plopped down in her favorite chair. "What's goin' on? You haven't popped up for a visit like this since before you got married."

I sat down on the sofa and dropped my purse on the floor. "Um, you know how I have to take those anger management classes, right?"

"Um-hmm," Mama said, her eyes glued to the TV.

"Well, we were doing an exercise tonight, and I remembered something from my childhood. Something I haven't thought about in a while. Something that can explain my anger issues."

"Um-hmm, what was it?"

"I remembered something about my father and Farrah."

Her head snapped in my direction. "You remembered *what*?"

"I remember my daddy, Calvin Weaver, putting his hands on Farrah."

Mama was silent.

"I remember I was ten, and she was four. I remember him sitting on the side of her bed in our room. I remember her crying, and when I sat up in the bed, he told me to lie back down and go to sleep."

Not a word from Mama.

"I remember I didn't really understand what was going on. I couldn't see what he was doing to her, but it sounded like he was hurting her."

Mama kept her focus on the TV.

"And I remember telling you what I saw."

She cleared her throat and sighed.

"Do you remember what you told me, Mama?"

"That was a long time ago, Alex, so I don't guess I do."

"You told me not to worry about it, that you'd take care of it. You also told me not to tell anybody else."

"Wasn't nobody else's business."

"What I don't understand is that night after night, for two years, he kept coming into our room, hurting Farrah—even after I told you. You didn't do anything, did you?"

She looked over at me, a cold expression on her face. "I talked to him, and he told me to mind my business, or he was gonna leave us. So I minded my business."

I frowned. This couldn't have been *my* mother, the woman I'd always looked up to. *My rock.* "You... you just *let* him do that to her?"

"I ain't never worked a day in my life. I did what I had to do to keep a roof over our heads and food in our stomachs."

"Mama, you let him molest her! How can you justify that?! No wonder she's so crazy!"

"I did the best I could in the situation. You have no right to sit there and judge me. He never messed with you, anyway. Why are you so upset?"

"Because she's my sister! And she's *your* daughter!"

"Well, what was I supposed to do, Alex? Call the police? Have him arrested? Then what? Move into a homeless shelter?"

"We could've made it. We were fine after he left."

"We were fine because of alimony and child support. We wouldn't have got that if he'd been locked up."

"You should've taken a chance. God would've provided. Your family would've helped."

Mama turned her whole body towards me. "Let me tell you something, girl. You ain't got no right to sit over there and judge me like you been living your life so right. Shoot, you hired that foreign boy to marry you."

My jaw dropped. How did she know that?

"That's right, *I know*. You put so much trust in your friend, Gwin; that girl's just like an old refrigerator, can't keep nothing. She's been spreading your business for years, told me a couple of days after you and Victor came over here for the party."

I have to admit that I was taken aback by what she'd said, but I also knew it was a ploy to get me to change the subject. I wasn't going to let her succeed. "That doesn't make what you did right. You should've been there for Farrah and for me."

"Everything ain't about right and wrong! Some things are about survival. I was just trying to make it. My only alternative was to move back home with my folks with two kids to take care of."

I shook my head and fought back the frustration that threatened to turn into rage. "Why did he leave, Mama? Did you finally say something to him? Tell him to stop?" I wanted so badly for that to be the case.

"He left because he found something better, I guess. I never asked. He came home one day and said he was leaving. I was too relieved to care why."

I sat there and looked at my mother and wondered how I had ever thought she was a good mother. How had I managed to push something so hideous and ugly out of my mind?

We sat in strained silence as I had no idea what to say or how to feel other than disgusted by her words and actions. Rage welled up inside of me. My hands trembled involuntarily. I pressed them to the sofa to steady them. I was trying to calm the racing of my heart when the front door flew open, and Farrah walked in.

"Mama, you left the front door unlocked. I just dropped by, because I thought I saw Alex's car in the driveway, but I know it can't be hers. She don't come around no more since she married that Brazilian Casanova she's so doggone proud—" She cut her own words off when she entered the living room and saw me sitting on the couch.

"Oh, so you *are* here," she said in a snide tone. "And you look like you mad, too. What? You gonna kick Mama's tail now?"

"I'm pretty sure she wants to," Mama muttered.

Farrah leaned against the door facing. "What did you do, Mama? Say *Victor's* name? She don't like that."

I looked up at Farrah and tried to control the tremor in my voice. "No, we were talking about you and Daddy."

Farrah's face fell as she stood there with a suddenly slumped posture.

"I was telling Mama that I remembered what he... what he used to do to you," I continued.

Farrah's eyes dropped to the floor.

"Do you remember, Farrah?" I asked.

She looked up at me with sad eyes. "Remember? I never forgot," she said in a tiny voice.

I shifted my eyes from Farrah to Mama. "I'm sorry for not helping you more, Farrah. I tried, but I should've done more."

Nothing from Farrah or Mama.

"I understand you now, why you are the way you are. Why Mama always caters to you. She thinks she can make up for what she let happen by keeping your kids and giving you money. And I spent my life trying to please her, overachieving just so I could get a little attention. I was wasting my time. She was too busy trying to fix her own mess with you."

Farrah frowned at me. "What are you talking about? Mama didn't know. I never told her."

"*I* told her. The first time I saw him… I told her, Farrah, and she chose to do nothing, because she needed him to pay the bills."

"You're lying!" Farrah shouted.

"No, I'm not. Mama just admitted it before you came in here. Tell her, Mama."

Mama shook her head. "I'm not gon' sit up here and study on ancient history with you, Alexandria Weaver. You need to let this go!" And with that, she stood from her seat and walked down the hall to her bedroom.

"You are so stupid! Why would you sit here and lie on Mama like that?! I hate you, I swear I do!" Farrah ranted.

I stood from the sofa. "I know you hate me, and now I understand why. But I'm telling you, I tried to help you. And I can still feel the frustration I felt as a little girl, because I felt so powerless back then. I tried. I really tried." I blinked back bitter tears.

Tears spilled from Farrah's eyes. "That's not why I hate you, Alex. I hate you because he never touched you. He never bothered you. It was always me. I used to wonder what I did that was so bad, bad enough to make him want to do that to me. There you were, in the same room, and he never messed with you. *That's* why I hate you!"

I reached for her, and she backed away from me. "I'm sorry, Farrah. For everything."

"That's why I slept with Quincy! And you know what? That wasn't the first or the last time. We've been messing around for years. I was sleeping with him before he became my lawyer."

I stood there with my mouth agape. Was she telling the truth, or was this just her anger talking?

"Close your mouth. I can't believe you didn't know. I mean, how could you think I could afford his services? I paid him in the bedroom. You know why he wouldn't set a date? Because he don't love you, you cow! He loves me. He was just using you!"

"Look, I know you're mad at me, so I'm going to leave now before you go overboard with the lies." I tried to move past her, but she blocked me. "*Move*, Farrah," I ordered.

She rolled her neck and her eyes. "Or, what? You gon' beat me down again? You better think twice about that, because you better believe I'm calling the popo if you touch me again, and this time you are going to jail to stay!"

I rolled my eyes and crossed my arms at my chest.

"Q and me met years ago at this party where successful men can meet women, and women like me can meet a man with more that ambition in his pocket. We hit it off real quick. It didn't matter to either of us that I was married. After all, Dequan was a loser anyway. The first time Quincy met you, you know what he said to me? 'Now, that's the kind of woman you marry—fat and desperate.'"

I felt my temper rising, but willed myself not to punch her in the nose.

"He said he loved me, but that you had more potential. So he dumped me. I was really mad about that, but he kept seeing me from time to time, and he helped me pay my bills as long as I kept quiet about me and him. Then you showed up and caught us that day, and he decided to kick me to the curb. He said he wasn't missing out on being with you with all the money you were making from the books and TV shows and stuff. That really hurt, because I love Q, you know?"

"Well, he's available now. Go for it," I said.

She laughed wryly. "No, he's not. He's still running in behind you and your money. I mean, for a while we were good again, and he had decided to leave you alone. But then you married Victor, and he couldn't stand the thought of another man spending your money after all the years he put in with you."

"Why are you telling me all of this now, Farrah? I'm not with Q anymore. I have a husband, a family. I don't care about Quincy."

"Did Q tell you about me and Victor?"

I felt a lump in my throat. "Yes, he told me he believes you and Victor were together."

"That's because I told him about me and Victor being together. We *were* together, Alex."

I nodded. "I see."

"You don't care?"

"Yes, I do care, Farrah, but there's nothing I can do about it now, and he doesn't even remember it. Look, I'm just trying to live my life and raise my daughters. I'm sorry you hate me. I'm sorry you think I got some type of special treatment, but the truth is, I was hurt by what he did, too. Not nearly as much as you, I know. But it affected me. It still does. I love you, Farrah. I really do. And I'm sorry."

As I walked towards the door, she shouted, "It was a lie!"

I stopped and turned to face her. "No, it's the truth. I told Mama about what Daddy did to you. She just didn't do anything about it."

"I'm not talking about that. That actually makes sense. It does explain how she's always been with me. And there was this one time I swear I saw her standing in the doorway when he did it, but I decided my mind was playing tricks on me. Now, I know it wasn't. She *was* standing there."

"I'm sorry, Farrah."

"I meant, I was lying about Victor. We were never together. I mean, I tried, but he wouldn't touch me."

I frowned. "But... but your perfume. I smelled it on him."

"You really know nothing about me. I don't wear perfume, I wear body oils. If you smelled anything on me, it was that. Everything I said about Q was true, but not Victor. That was just a story Quincy cooked up to get you to leave Victor so he could get back with you."

"Why would you go along with all of this stuff for Q, Farrah, if in the end he was planning to marry me?"

"Because he promised he'd only be married to you long enough to earn the right to get some of your money in the divorce, and then we were gonna be together."

I nodded. "Well, I'll say this: you two belong together. I'm sorry for what happened to you when we were girls, but I never want to see you again."

"Yeah, well, go on home to your fake husband and live your little fake life, then," she snorted.

I shook my head. "Mama told you?"

"Nope, Q told me. Pillow talk."

I tilted my head to the side, looked at my sister for what I hoped was the last time, and left my mother's house.

27

"Tha Crossroads"

I walked into my house with a heavy heart and mind. The revelations from my mother and my sister had cracked the foundation of everything I believed. I didn't even feel like Alex Weaver anymore. I had no idea who I was, actually. My identity had been totally destroyed. I sighed woefully as I slowly walked through the quiet darkness and sat down on my sofa. I sat there and stared at nothing for a minute or two, and then I balled up my hands and punched the pillows on my sofa until my arms were sore.

And when my energy was gone, I lay on the sofa, curled myself up into a ball, closed my eyes tightly, and cried silent tears. Moments later, I felt Victor sit down beside me. He lifted my head from the sofa and rested it in his lap. Then he softly stroked my hair and began to whisper to me: "Não chore, querida. Não chore. Do not cry." He whispered the words over and over again.

The sensation of his touch and the sound of his voice soothed me. In a matter of minutes, my tears ceased as I soaked up his comfort.

"Do you want to talk about it?" he asked after a few moments of quiet.

I nodded slightly, my head still in his lap.

He bent over and kissed my cheek. "Tell me, querida."

I sucked in a breath and slowly released it. "Tonight, at my class, I remembered… or realized some things about my childhood that I had buried a long time ago. And after class, I went to talk to my mother about them, about what my father did to my sister, and she acted like it didn't matter. She... she let him do things to my sister. She didn't stop him. I don't know how to feel about that, Victor. She's not who I thought she was. I named our daughter after her, and now I wish I could change it."

"Ruby is a good child. No name can change that. And it was long ago that this happened, yes?"

"Yes, but she acts like it was nothing. She actually thinks she was right to let him do that stuff. I don't know if I can ever see her in the same light again. I don't know if I can ever forgive her."

"We are not so different, querida, and neither are our mothers. If I can forgive my mother, you can forgive yours."

"I'm not you, Victor. And even if I do forgive her, I don't know if I'll ever be able to be in the same room with her again."

"Then, so be it. Never talk to her again, but forgive her."

I was quiet for a moment, then I said, "And Farrah said some horrible things to me—about my relationship with Quincy. She said it was all a lie, and although she's the biggest liar in Texas, I think I believe her. And then I found out that Gwin's been spreading my business to anyone who'll listen. I just feel like everyone I trusted and cared about has stabbed me in the back."

"I did not know you cared so much for this Quincy."

"I... I don't, anymore, but we were together for eight years. That's a long time to be with someone and find out they were pretending to like you."

"I see," he said, his voice strained.

"I don't know what to do, Victor."

"What do you want to do?"

"Honestly, I want to cancel the dedication, fly to Brazil, and never come back here. There's nothing here for me anymore."

He sighed. "The dedication is important for the girls, yeah?"

"Yes, it is, but we can have the ceremony at your uncle's church in São Paulo."

"No, you have already made plans for your church. We can have the dedication and leave for Brazil as planned, but instead of staying a short while, we never have to come back."

I looked up at him. "You really think we could do that?"

"What can stop us, minha querida?" he asked, his eyes locked with mine.

I closed my eyes. "Nothing."

***

When the day of the dedication arrived, I felt both relieved and apprehensive. Relieved because this would be the last time I'd have to be in the same room with my mother or Gwin or Farrah. Apprehensive because I'd be in the same room with my mother and Gwin and Farrah. I hadn't talked to either of them in more than a week. I'd dodged their calls and changed the locks on my door to prevent any unwanted pop-up visits. I spent that time planning my family's move to Brazil, working things out with my probation officer, and completing my anger management classes. Just two days after the dedication, we would be leaving Houston for good.

I was convinced things would be better there. I could still write and manage my business affairs from there. The girls would grow up around Victor's family. And Victor could resume his old job—sans the gigolo services, of course.

As I peered at myself in the mirror, I silently prayed that this day would race by and that neither of the people I'd been avoiding would approach me. Surely by now they'd gotten the message that I wanted nothing to do with them.

I gave myself a final once over in the mirror—hair, *check*. Make-up, *check*, dress, *check*, fake smile, *check*. I was all ready to go. I met Victor in the hallway holding onto Ruby's hand with Daisy in his arms. They looked good together, the three of them—father and daughters. I smiled as I led the way down the stairs, out of the house, and to the car.

The dedication ceremony was scheduled for right before the sermon, so we wouldn't have to wait too long. That was good, because little Miss Ruby wasn't good at sitting still for long periods of time. When the girls' names were finally announced, I was so relieved I almost ran up to the platform. Once Victor, the girls, and I were in place, Elder Pointer invited our other family members and friends to join us in laying hands on the girls. As I stood there and watched my family members approach the platform, I felt my stomach began to bubble—especially when my mother approached us with a huge smile on her face. She was followed by a few of my cousins and my Aunt Nancy. Gwin and her daughter, Amiya, followed as did Farrah. The only thought running through my mind was that I should've never invited any of them. This whole thing was a mistake.

Upon instructions from Elder Pointer, I closed my eyes and bowed my head as she began to pray:

"We are gathered here today to give back to God what He has gifted to Victor and Alexandria. We commit these beautiful little girls to God. We pray right now that Daisy and Ruby will know the true goodness of God for all the days of their lives. We ask You to cover these girls, Lord. To bless them with gifts and talents to further Your kingdom. Bless them to lead Godly lives and let their light shine wherever they may go. We pray that they will be blessings to their parents, their family, and the entire world..."

As I stood there in front of the church, head bowed, eyes closed, I thought about the hypocrites surrounding me. My blood boiled at the fact that these people were touching my daughters, smiles plastered on their faces, their mouths full of false well wishes. If there was anything I hated, it was a liar and a coward. Farrah and Gwin were liars. My mother was a coward. What despicable people I had surrounded myself with.

What about you? Are you not a liar? A coward? My own thoughts were turning against me. I slightly shook my head in response. Who had I lied to? What was I afraid of?

And my conscience answered with one single word: *Victor*. I was lying to him, pretending we had built our marriage on love. I was afraid to tell him the truth, afraid to lose him. Yes, I was just as bad as the people who'd hurt me, if not worse. At least their lies had been revealed. I was still hiding behind mine.

I opened my eyes and looked up at Victor. I loved him. I *really* loved him, and I loved us as a family. I finally had what I'd always wanted. And he loved me, too. But what did he love? The lies I let him believe were true? His idea of what we were? If I faced the truth, I'd see that I was just like Mama and Farrah and Gwin and Quincy. I was pretending to be something I wasn't. I was pretending I hadn't brokered our marriage like a business deal. And I was doing all of this pretending, because I thought I finally had what I wanted—love and a family. But it wasn't real.

It wasn't real.

I gave Elder Pointer a watered down smile when she handed me the gift Bibles for the girls, but my heart was aching. As we left the platform and headed to our seats, I felt a heaviness in my spirit that nearly brought me to tears. The feeling wasn't helped by the fact that Quincy was standing in the back of the church staring at me.

I sighed heavily as we reclaimed our seats. Victor looked over at me and took my hand in his, squeezing it tightly.

"Is something wrong?" he whispered.

I shook my head and focused on the pastor as she began to bring the day's message. Or at least I pretended to focus, because I actually didn't hear a word she said. Too many thoughts crowded my mind, and my own guilt consumed my heart.

After service, I grabbed Daisy and quickly made my way out of the sanctuary, leaving poor Victor behind to face the well-wishers alone. I secured Daisy in her car seat and climbed into the passenger's seat. I turned the key in the ignition so that the cool air could flow through the car in the spring sun as I waited for Victor. I closed my eyes and rested my head against the seat, feeling a little less anxious. That feeling fled when I heard a tap on my window and saw Quincy standing next to my car. I did the only thing I knew to do in response. I closed my eyes and acted like he wasn't there, hoping he would take the hint and go away.

After a couple more taps, I heard a muffled, "I just wanted to say congratulations."

I didn't open my eyes or move a muscle. A few minutes later, I heard another muffled voice. Victor's. "Unlock the door, querida."

In no time, we were on our way home. Victor didn't ask any questions until we were back home, and the girls were down for their afternoon nap.

I was in the kitchen preparing dinner when he approached me. "You do not want me to cook?" he asked. I guess it was odd for me to be in the kitchen since cooking had been his job almost since the second he returned home.

"No, I got it," I replied without turning to face him.

He walked over to me and stood behind me. I could feel the heat from his body as he rested his hands on my shoulders. "Talk to me."

I sighed and turned to face him. I reached up and softly kissed his lips. "Okay."

We sat at the kitchen table, and for a moment, I just looked at him and planted his face in my memory. I tried to talk myself out of telling him the truth, but my sensible side won out.

"Victor, I need to tell you something. It… it's very important. It's about us, me and you, and how we were before you got hurt and lost your memory."

His eyes were full of questions as he nodded and said, "All right."

I sighed deeply. "First, I need to tell you that I love you, Victor. I really do. Please know that."

He smiled. "And I love you."

I shook my head. "No, you just *think* you do, because I never told you any different."

Creases formed in his brow. "What? No, I love you, querida. I *do*."

"Victor, do you remember what your job was in Rio?"

He nodded slightly. "Yes."

"I'm not talking about giving massages. I'm talking about your *other* job."

He dropped his eyes and softly said, "Yes."

"Then you know that women paid you for your time."

"Yes."

"When I met you in Rio, I was feeling really bad about myself and my life, and you helped me feel better. I didn't pay you then, but I did pay you to marry me. We signed a contract and everything." I pulled my purse from the table and dug into it until I found the envelope that held our marriage contract. I laid it before him. "The terms were fulfilled after I had Daisy. Technically, you are free to divorce me now. I'm sorry I let you think we had a real marriage with real love. But honestly, I did grow to love you, Victor. You just never loved me."

Victor silently stared down at the papers.

"I… I was so afraid to tell you the truth, because I didn't want to lose you, but I was just as afraid you'd remember on your own and leave anyway. I don't know what's more pathetic, me being so desperate for your love that I'd be willing to live a lie, or the fact that you had to forget me to even think you loved me."

His eyes drifted from the paper to my face, hurt evident in them. "Alexandria… I…"

"You remember now, don't you?"

He nodded.

"I'm sorry for not being honest with you at first. I just… I love you *so much*, more than I have any other man, and I really wanted to be with you." I shook my head. "I'm so pitiful."

I kept my eyes fixed on the table, and there was an almost eerie silence between us for several minutes. I could hear Victor breathe. I could hear the light traffic outside my house. I could hear the water in the pot as it began to boil, and then I heard the sound of paper tearing. I looked up to see Victor ripping the contract into shreds.

"What are you doing?" I asked.

He stood from the table and dropped the paper shreds into the boiling pot. "What does it look like I am doing?"

"Victor—"

He squatted beside my chair. "I remembered long ago, querida. It does not matter. None of it matters anymore."

"You... you *remembered*? When?"

"I remembered you the moment you walked into that hospital room."

I stared down at him with wide eyes. "You never had amnesia?"

"I did, but the memories came back a few at a time until I saw you. Then everything came back at once. You healed me, Alexandria."

I stood from the table, feeling very confused and extremely stupid at the same time. "It was... it was all an act?! You *pretended* not to remember me or Ruby or your mother?! Why would you do that?!"

He stood to face me. "Have you not been happy?"

"Yes, but it was all based on a lie! I thought you didn't remember me!"

"I am telling you the truth now."

"You played with me. I bet you laughed at me all the time behind my back. I feel like such a fool..."

"No! I... I love you, Alexandria. I truly do. I have loved you for a long time. I think I fell in love with you the first time I held you in my arms—when you cried. In Rio."

I stared at him and tried to decide if he was telling the truth. It was no use. I wouldn't know the truth if it walked up to me and slapped me in the face. "Why didn't you just tell me? Why did you cheat on me and disappear on me? You hurt me. That's not love."

"Would you have believed me if I told you? Would you have accepted my hand in marriage if I had professed my love to you in Rio, if I had said I was tired of my life and I wanted something real and true?"

I shifted my eyes from him and remained silent.

"Of course not. You are not the kind of woman who believes in love at first sight or soul mates. Everything with you has to be planned."

"You don't know a thing about me! You don't know what I believe in!"

"I know you had no trouble marrying me when you thought I did not love you, when you thought it was only a business deal. You never cared about how I felt for you until you felt love for me. You never would have married me if I had told you I loved you from the moment I first saw you. You would not have believed me."

"That's not true," I said softly.

"Yes, it is. What Quincy and your sister did to you ruined you."

"You're the one who kept talking about business and pleasure. You're the one who said it wouldn't be a marriage of love!"

"I said what I thought you needed to hear."

I shook my head. "That doesn't make any sense. So you thought I needed you to be unfaithful, too? Is that it?"

He stepped closer to me. I stepped back. "I was not unfaithful, Alexandria. From the moment we took vows, I've been true to you. There were no other women. I am tired of other women."

"And I'm supposed to believe that? You disappeared for a week! And before that, you kept coming home smelling like perfume or body oil or something."

"Perfume?"

"Yes, *perfume*. The same fragrance my sister wears, though she says it's body oil."

Victor's frown turned into a smile, and his smile turned into light laughter.

"At least you're laughing *in* my face this time," I said as I collapsed back into the chair and rested my head on the table.

"No… no, wait here," he said.

I looked up to see him racing from the kitchen. If I didn't fear being locked away from my daughters, I would've grabbed that pot of boiled paper from the stove and been poised to dash it on him when he returned to the kitchen. But instead, I sat there at the table with my forehead pressed into the wood, feeling, and probably looking, like the biggest idiot in the world.

I looked up again when I heard and felt something thud against the top of the table. It was a case, and when Victor opened it, I saw that it was full of massage oils—body oils.

He removed the bottles one by one, uncapping each of them and setting them before me on the table. "Is any of this what you smelled?"

I sat up, tested the oils, and tapped the third bottle. "This one. I've, uh… never seen these before."

"I know. I bought them for work and never used them on you. All of those nights I came home late, I was working. I did not want to face you, so I just worked as much as I could. I was not unfaithful."

I shrugged, not to be outdone. "It wouldn't matter if you were. Our marriage was fake anyway."

He sat down across from me. "You see, it was words like those that confused me, Alexandria. You tell me you love me, and then you throw the condition of our marriage at me, remind me to play my role. Then there was Quincy. He was always around, knocking at our door, and you never seemed to know if you wanted him in or out of your life. I knew I loved you, but I was never really certain how you felt about me."

"But I *told* you, Victor. I told you how I felt, and you turned away from me."

"I know, and I am sorry. I just did not know how to deal with what I was feeling for you. I loved you, and I wanted to be with you, but I was afraid of hurting you. I did not think I was any good for you, and I was afraid you would always see me as a whore, because that is the way I always see myself."

"I won't lie, at first I saw things strictly from a business standpoint and maybe a sexual one, too, but you made me love you with your kindness and attention. You really did."

He smiled slightly. "You made me love you, too. When I saw your pain and felt your heart in Rio, you made me love you. I had never felt so connected to a woman before. We are bound to each other, querida, heart to heart. *I love you.*"

I felt my heart skip a beat, rested my hand on my chest. "Then…

then why did you disappear without a word for a whole week?"

He sighed. "I... I do not know. I was trying to decide what to do. When I was around you, I wanted to hold you and love you, but I thought it was best to keep my distance. Then there were times I could not resist being with you and touching you. And I would feel guilty about it. My mind was... I do not know. I thought it was best to leave. But after a week, I had to come back to you, because of my love for you."

We were silent for a while. Then Victor spoke. "Do you want me to leave? Are you still coming to Brazil?"

I thought for a moment, then said, "I appreciate you for being honest with me now, but I don't think it would do us any good to stay together. Too many lies have been told, and too many games have been played. You can use your ticket to go back home, but I won't be joining you."

Genuine disappointment shadowed his face. "What about the girls?"

"You can see them whenever you want."

"In Brazil?"

"Yes, I'll bring them to see you, but not now. I need... I need time."

He nodded as he stood from the chair. "I understand, and I am sorry."

I held my head in my hands. "Where will you go? Your flight isn't for a couple of days."

"I will try to trade the ticket for an earlier flight. If not, I will sleep in the airport. I do not want to be any more of a bother to you." He bent over and kissed my cheek. "If you change your mind, you know my number and my mother's number."

I stood to my feet. "Wait, how are you getting to the airport?"

He moved closer to me. "Do not worry about me, querida. I'll take a taxi."

I dropped my eyes. I was so conflicted. In my heart, I wanted him to stay. In my mind, I knew it was best for him to leave. "Okay," I said barely above a whisper.

"Can I say something before I go?" he asked.

I nodded slightly.

"When I was in the hospital, there was so much pain, so much fear, and when the nurses and doctors told me what happened to me, what those men did to me, I hated them, though I did not know who they were. I wished them dead, Alexandria. But now... now I am thankful for what they did. I do not care if they are ever caught. It does not matter, because what they did to me gave me another chance to love you and to do it the way you deserve. To be a good husband to you and a good father to my children." He smiled at me as he stroked my cheek. "I made mistakes, and I hurt you. For that I am sorry, but I love you. I was not sure how to show you or tell you before, but I love you with all of my heart. I always have. I always will."

I looked up at him, into those hypnotic, amber eyes and said, "I love you, too."

He kneeled before me, took my hand, and placed it on his chest. "It beats for you. I think it always has."

I stared at him as he stood and kissed both of my cheeks.

Then I watched him leave.

28

"Can We Talk"

"Thank you so much for coming over. I... I didn't know where else to turn," I said as I wiped tears.

Elder Pointer nodded. "Well, you sounded desperate on the phone."

"I *am* desperate, but still, I know this was a sacrifice for you, leaving the church to come here and see me. Especially with the way I went about doing things—not counseling with you before my marriage."

Elder Pointer, who was dressed in a black skirt and matching blouse, said, "Well, I'm not here to judge you, Alex. I'm here to help you."

"And I'm sorry you had to come all the way over here, but like I said on the phone, I don't have anyone to watch the girls. Otherwise, I would've come to the church."

"It's quite all right. Now, what's on your mind?"

I looked down at Daisy, who was fast asleep in my lap, and at Ruby, who was napping next to me on the sofa. Then I looked back at Elder Pointer and began to bare my soul. I told all that I'd done or had been done to me—from my father's abuse of Farrah and my mother's indifference, to my relationship with Victor and everything and everyone in between.

She sat and listened to every word as I droned on and on about my feelings of hurt and pain. When I cried, she walked over to me and rested her hand on my shoulder. When I became angry, she spoke words to calm me. When I was finally quiet, she began to counsel me.

"You've been through quite a lot. Some bad things have happened, but also, some good things have happened. You have two beautiful miracles that came out of all that happened to you."

I nodded. "Yes, I thank God for my babies."

"But there is a lot that's bothering you. Your father, Farrah, your mother?"

"Yes. I feel so bad for Farrah—like I should've done more to help her."

"Alex, you were a child. What were you supposed to do other than what you did?"

"After I told my mother and she didn't do anything, I… I should've told someone else. I should've told my aunt or someone."

Elder Pointer shook her head as she took my hand and squeezed it. "Alex, you were a child, and Farrah's well-being was not your responsibility. You did what you were supposed to do—the only thing you *could* do. What happened to her was not your fault."

"What about afterwards? I just went on with my life and acted like it didn't happen. All the while, Farrah's had to carry this alone all these years."

"That was your mind's way of dealing with it, of coping with it and protecting you from the pain. Just like Farrah's behavior is how she deals with it. And don't forget, you carried it in your own way with the way you handled, or mishandled, your anger. Now you've confronted it and offered your empathy to her, and that's a good thing." Elder Pointer's voice was so calm and soothing, like icy water on a balmy summer's day.

I nodded. "What about my mother? How can I make her see what she's done?"

"Well, dear, you can't make another person do anything."

"Then what am I supposed to do?"

"Pray for her and forgive her, but most of all, forgive yourself."

"Forgive? I'm just supposed to forgive? Am I supposed to forgive everyone? My father, Quincy, Gwin?"

"And Farrah and Victor, yes."

"How? After what they've done, the way they hurt me?"

"How? You see their side of things, and you reach deep inside of yourself and see where in some instances, you held some responsibility for what happened. Then you remember that God forgives without prejudice."

I shook my head. "I'm not God."

"No, but you are His child, Alex, and inside of you is the same power that raised Christ from the dead. And with that power, you can do anything—*including* forgiving those who hurt you. I'm sure those anger management classes have been helpful, but true deliverance can only come from God. He is the only one who can help you keep your anger in check. But He can't deliver you unless you forgive. And remember, forgiveness is not for the person you forgive, but for *you*. Bitterness eats away at your soul and leaves a big hole in your heart. You don't need to carry that around with you. You've got your children to take care of, and you've got to make a decision about your marriage."

"I... I've already made that decision. I can't be with him. Our relationship started out wrong and became more wrong as time passed. It'll never work."

"Well, before you make that decision, you should pray. Just because you didn't consult God before the marriage doesn't mean you can't consult Him now. He's always waiting and willing to hear from you. And just because your marriage began in an unorthodox manner doesn't mean it can't be saved. One thing I do suggest, though, is that you make sure Victor is saved. If he isn't, pray for his salvation, whether you reconcile with him or not."

I nodded. "Yes, ma'am."

"And let me say this: judging from what I saw at the girls' dedication, there's a bond shared between you and your husband. There's something special there. Something worth salvaging. I'm sure others can see it, too. I believe the two of you have loved each other for a long while, but you were both too broken to realize it or to accept it."

I smiled at her words, but I was still unsure about things with Victor. "Thank you for telling me that."

"You're welcome, dear. Well, I'm due back in my office in a little while. Let me pray with you before I go."

I nodded as Elder Pointer tightly gripped my hand and began to pray: "Heavenly Father, we come to You this glorious day as humbly as we know how. First we want to thank You, Father, for allowing us to see this day. For Your grace and mercy. For Your kindness and faithfulness. Lord, I know that You already know what Your child, Alexandria, stands in need of. She needs to feel Your presence and know that Your loving arms of comfort are wrapped around her. She needs Your guidance, Lord, and Your forgiveness. But most of all, she needs the power to forgive herself. In Jesus' name we pray, amen."

I opened my eyes and lifted my head. "Amen. Thank you, Pastor. Thank you so much."

She smiled at me and patted my hand. "You're welcome. My door is always open, and if you're still having childcare issues, I'm more than willing to come back over. You need only call me. Okay?"

I returned her smile with a small one of my own. "Okay."

***

I missed Victor. It had been a week since he left, and I missed him terribly. I missed his presence, his touch, his cooking. I missed the way he smelled. I missed his smile. I missed his love. And though he called every day to check on the girls, I missed his voice. I missed his arms around me. I just missed *him*.

I looked over at the plane tickets that lay on my coffee table, the tickets to Brazil that Ruby and Daisy and I hadn't used. I shouldn't have let him go, or at least I should've gone with him.

I loved him.

I closed my eyes and began to pray about Victor and my feelings for him: "Lord, show me what to do. I miss him so much. I know I love him, but I'm not sure if I should believe that he loves me. I'm so confused…"

Once I'd finished praying, I sat there and listened to my girls playing on the floor and tried to hear God's voice in my head. But instead, I heard a knock at my door. I walked to the door and checked the peep hole and couldn't believe my eyes. Standing there was Quincy, flowers in hand.

"What the?" I whispered.

I stood there for several minutes as he continued to knock. Then I decided to ignore him. I knew I had no business talking to Quincy in my current mental state. I missed my husband, and my crazy mind might've turned that into missing Quincy. Besides, what did we have left to talk about?

I returned to the living room and watched my girls. Ruby was jumping up and down to some music on the TV, and Daisy was lying on the floor watching her big sister. I smiled at them. They were both so much like Victor—beautiful and full of life. Then I heard the sound of a fist banging against thick glass. I rushed to the patio doors to find Quincy beating frantically on the glass.

"Stop that!" I shouted through the closed doors. "You're gonna scare my babies."

"Then let me in," he said in a muffled voice.

"No, go away!"

Daisy began to whimper. Evidently, *I* had frightened her.

More knocking at the patio doors.

I snatched them open and went to pick Daisy up. I cradled her in my arms and soothed her as I took a seat on the sofa. Quincy slowly walked into the room and closed the door behind him. "I should've locked the doggone gate," I said.

"Is your husband home?"

"No, what do you want?"

"I need to talk to you," he said as he sat down beside me.

I sighed. "What about?"

"Us?"

"There is no *us*. Farrah told me about the long love affair you two've been having and how the only thing you've ever really wanted from me is my money. It's truly over between us. I'm just trying to work on forgiving you now."

"I know you don't believe Farrah! Come on, now, Alex. *Farrah?*"

I looked at the floor. "Yes, I believe her. At least I believe *some* of what she said."

He threw up his hands. "Why?! You know that girl loves to lie, and she loves to hurt you."

I looked over at him. "Okay, look me in the eye, and tell me that you were only with her once."

He stared at me and with a straight face said, "I was only with her once, Alex. And it was a mistake, and for the millionth time, *I'm sorry.*"

I nodded and sat there and thought about my conversation with Elder Pointer. *This* was my part in things going wrong with Quincy. I gave him chance after chance. I kept falling for his words.

"You know what, Q?" I began. "I shouldn't have asked you that, because it doesn't matter. The truth is, whether you slept with her once or a zillion times, we can't be together. But I'm not angry at you. I understand I let some things happen between us. I sat around for eight years, never really believing that you loved me, giving myself to you time and time again, settling for less than I deserved. And then I decided to forgive you for sleeping with Farrah while refusing to forgive her, and that was just backwards and crazy and silly. I should've been done with you long ago. Maybe Farrah is lying, and maybe she's not. I just don't care anymore."

"That's it? You're just going to throw what we had away and keep up this fake life you've made with that dude?"

"You know, Quincy? What I do from here on out is absolutely none of your business. Now please see yourself out, and have a nice life."

"You don't love me anymore?"

"Give it up, Q."

"Do you?"

I sighed. "I love you as a brother in Christ."

"That's all?"

"Yes."

He sat there for a minute as if letting my words sink in. Then he broke into an impromptu confessional. "Okay. Um, for what it's worth, I do love you."

"Mm-hmm. Well, for what it's worth, the love I once had for you does not even compare to the love I have for my *fake* husband. Now, feel free to call Farrah and have a good laugh about that. Bye, Quincy."

He stood and slowly walked out the patio door. I locked it behind him, glad that chapter of my life was finally over.

My first thought was to call Gwin and tell her what happened. Then I remembered I hadn't spoken to her in a couple of weeks, because I was mad at her. Then I remembered I was supposed to be learning to forgive.

I sighed and followed my first mind. I took both Daisy and Ruby into the kitchen for a snack. Then I sat at the table and called Gwin on my cell phone. It rang three times before I heard her uncertain "hello."

"Hey, Gwin? It's Alex."

"Wow, I was beginning to wonder if I'd ever get to talk to you again. You flew out of the church so fast after the girls' dedication, I didn't get a chance to talk to you, and you won't answer your phone or your door, and you changed your locks."

"Yeah, I needed some time. I was really upset."

"With me? Why?"

I sighed. "Have you spoken to my mother lately?"

"Now that you mention it, I haven't been able to get in touch with her, either. Alex, what's going on?"

I felt kind of bad for shutting her out of my life without explaining why. She'd been my friend since grade school. I owed her more courtesy than that. "Look, are you busy right now? Can you come over?"

"Are you gonna let me in?"

"Of course I am."

"Then I'm on my way."

By the time Gwin made it to my house, I'd put both of the girls to bed, but the first words out of her mouth when she walked through the door were, "Where are the girls?" So I took her to their room and let her peek in on them.

"I've missed them," she said softly. She reached for my hand. "And I've missed you, Alex."

I smiled and grasped her hand. "I've missed you, too."

We headed down the stairs to the kitchen where I poured us both a glass of iced tea. We settled down at the table and sipped our drinks in silence.

When I got up to refill my glass, she said, "You're stalling. What is it?"

I took my seat and studied the tea and ice for a moment. "Mama told me something about you, something you did that really made me question our friendship."

Gwin frowned. "Miss Ruby? What did she tell you?"

I looked up at her. "She said you told her that my marriage was fake. She said you've been spreading my business for years."

Gwin's shoulders slumped as she dropped her eyes to the table. A full minute passed before she spoke. "I'm sorry," she simply said. Her eyes remained downcast.

"I forgive you, and I want to apologize for asking you to help me perpetrate a lie. And I want to take responsibility for all the years I sat up and listened to you talk about other people. I should've known if you'd spread their business, you'd spread mine, but I guess I thought I could trust you to keep what I told you in confidence, and it hurt to know that, to you, I was just like everyone else."

She shook her head. "No, you weren't. You were, and are, very special to me. We've shared a lot through the years, and I really am sorry, Alex. Maybe I have a problem or something. At least that's what my husband says."

I smiled a little. "Look, I love you, Gwin, and you'll always be my friend, but I can't lie and say we'll ever be as close as we once were. But I do forgive you, and I hope you forgive me."

A single tear rolled down her cheek. "Of course I forgive you, and thank you for forgiving me. I've missed you."

I looked at her for a moment and really wanted to tell her about the argument I'd had with Mama, but instead I said, "I've missed you, too."

29

"Stop The World"

I stood at my mother's front door, two babies in my arms, my breath caught in my throat. For so many years her home had been a haven to me, the one place I could go, no matter how I felt, and have my troubled mind or heart soothed by her words and her food and her comfort. But now it symbolized something else to me. It was the same house I'd grown up in—the scene of the crime. The place where my mother, my hero, had let my sister down and at the same time, let me down, too.

I rang the doorbell and waited. What if she refused to let me in this time? I hoped that wouldn't be the case, because I needed her in my life and my girls' lives. She and I needed to find a way to fix things between us.

She opened the door without shouting "Who is it?!" like she usually did. It was a running joke between us, because either she knew I was coming, because I'd called ahead, or she'd already checked the peep hole. Since I hadn't called, I knew she'd seen me through the peep hole.

"Hey, Mama," I said softly.

In response, she reached for her namesake, pulling her into her arms and then turning back into the house without a word to me. I followed her into the living room, and we took our regular seats. I sat Daisy in my lap and watched as Mama kissed Ruby's cheek and hugged her close to her body.

"I've missed you, little one," she said softly. "You and your sister both."

I turned my attention to the TV, which I don't think ever got much of a break in that house. It seemed like it was always on. At that moment, it was tuned to a broadcast of a Creflo Dollar sermon.

"Where's Mr. Wesley?" I asked, attempting to break the ice.

"Sleep," Mama answered. "Daisy is growing."

I nodded. "Like a weed. I think she's gonna be tall, like Victor."

"Yeah."

For the next ten minutes, only Creflo Dollar's voice filled the room, and when he was done, Joyce Meyer's voice took its place. I liked Joyce Meyer, but I wasn't there to watch her. I was there to talk to my mother.

"Mama, um, I think we should talk, you know, about the other week."

Mama kept her focus on Ruby, kissed her forehead.

"Mama—"

"I'm not gonna go through this again with you, Alex. I deserve some peace in my life now. I ain't gonna let you upset me today," she said, her eyes still on Ruby.

"Mama, I'm not trying to disturb your peace. I just want us to fix things."

"Fix things? What is there to fix? What's past is past. It happened, and now it's over; everybody has gone on with their lives. We all lived, and we are all fine. Let it be, Alex. Let it rest."

I tried to let her words sink in. She thought we were all okay. She thought *she* was okay. I sat there for a few minutes and looked at my mother, and for the first time in my life, I really saw her.

"I understand now," I said softly.

"Well, good," Mama said.

"I understand that I really can't imagine what it must've been like for you, how torn you were. How it must've felt to live life knowing what you know. I understand that this is how you've coped with things—by sweeping them under this big rug and walking all over it, ignoring the bumps and rough spots. I guess it was the only way you could deal with things. I understand that in your mind, you did the best you could.

"And I forgive you, Mama. I forgive you, and I ask that you forgive me for judging you. I have no idea what it feels like to be you, to face what you faced. But it hurts, because I always looked up to you. I always wanted to be like you, to be as strong as I thought you were. I lived my whole life trying to please you and make you proud of me, because I knew you'd been through so much with the divorce and all. I remember everything you taught me about men and love and marriage and being independent. I lived by it all—don't shack up, get married before you have children, be sure you can take care of yourself.

"I followed your advice, because I wanted to please you—not because it was the right thing to do. That's why I hired Victor. That's why I stayed with Quincy for so long. That's why I pushed him into setting a date. That's why I got the degree—to please *you*. I'm not blaming you. Those were my choices. But can't you see what remembering the truth of my childhood has done? It's made everything I ever did seem so stupid and wrong, because it was for *you*. I love you, Mama, but I am so disappointed."

I fell silent as tears filled my eyes. There were no more words to say, or at least nothing that would matter was left to say. I looked over at Mama, whose face was wet, but she didn't speak, either. She just hugged Ruby and cried silent tears.

We sat there for several more minutes before I stood from the sofa and balanced Daisy on my hip. "I guess I should go now," I said as I reached for Ruby.

Mama just sat there for a moment, her eyes fixed on the TV. When she spoke, her voice was so light, I barely heard her. "Farrah is not your daddy's child. I cheated on him."

I frowned and reclaimed my seat. Before I could respond, Mama began to speak again.

"He never forgave me for it, but he agreed to raise her as his own. I always figured what he did to her was my punishment, and I guess I thought I deserved it. So I let him do it, because I deserved it, and because I needed him to take care of us. And I loved him, and I didn't want to be alone.

"As time went on, I saw what it was doing to Farrah. She was such a sweet child at first, and then she just started to change. And I prayed to God to give me the strength to do something to stop him or to leave him. I prayed that prayer for two years, and when he finally left, I was so relieved. One day he came in from work and said he was leaving, that's it. No explanation, and I didn't ask no questions, because I knew it was God's way of doing what I was too weak to do."

She began to cry again. Part of me wanted to hug her, but I was stuck to that sofa. I just couldn't move. The mother in me, the protector of my daughters, couldn't really sympathize with her. Because I knew if anyone laid a hand on either of my girls—including Victor, whom I truly loved—I would tear them limb from limb. So I sat there and let her cry, and when she was done, I walked over to her and took Ruby from her.

As I turned to leave, she said, "You gonna tell Farrah what I told you? She thinks y'all got the same daddy."

I shook my head. "It's not for me to tell. That's up to you. I said what I needed to say to Farrah the other week. Nothing left to say. Nothing left for me to do but pray for her, for all of us. But, she has a right to know. It'll probably make her feel better to know he's not her father."

Mama nodded. "What about your daddy? You gonna confront him, too. After all, he's the one that did it."

I stood there for a moment and tried to think of a good answer for her. I honestly hadn't considered confronting him. "I don't know, maybe one day. But honestly, I haven't spoken to him in years. He hasn't been a part of my life since he left, and he wasn't much of a part of it when he was here. You were my world; he's a ghost to me. For all I know, he could be dead by now."

Mama was silent.

After a few minutes of standing there with nothing to say, I left, my heart a little lighter and a little heavier at the same time.

***

Having time alone with your thoughts and with God can reveal a lot to you about yourself. I learned that though I was successful in a lot of ways, I still lacked confidence in some areas. And I still feared failure. I guess that's why I followed up my failed relationships with Quincy with a fake one—one I believed would avoid failure. Of course, I'd failed anyway. In my case, it was true that the thing I feared the most was the thing I brought into my life.

I sat in my living room with my girls and thought about Victor, about how I'd fallen in love with him—with his kindness and charm—not realizing it was all an act, an act that was included in our contract. But he said he loved me, that he'd *always* loved me, that his heart beat for me. How could I believe him? *Should I believe him?* Could I take a chance on him, on our marriage?

I thumbed through my Bible, which had become my constant companion. I scanned the chapters and verses. I meditated on the words. And that's when it occurred to me. There was nothing in that Bible that said it was a sin to take a chance. The Bible was all about second and third and fourth chances. I was reminded of the sermon I'd heard at Gwin's church, that God is the God of infinite chances. I loved this man, and no matter how things between us had started, maybe we could make it work. Maybe what started out as fake had evolved into something real. Maybe there really was a bond between us like Elder Pointer and Victor had said. Maybe we deserved another chance. It had been weeks since he left, but maybe… just maybe…

I closed my eyes and whispered a short prayer: *"Please God, let this be the right decision."* Then I picked up my phone and dialed Victor's number. It rang straight to voicemail. I hung up and then decided to call back and leave a message.

"Hey, Victor, it's Alex… Alexandria. I miss you and I love you and I really don't want to be apart anymore. I'm… I'm going to bring the girls to Brazil to see you, and maybe we can talk then. Um, okay. Bye."

I started to call his mother, but decided my time would be better spent packing. He needed to see the girls whether we worked things out or not. So I took the girls upstairs, vowing with every step that if Victor and I were able to work things out and we lived together in Brazil, our home would only have one floor. I was tired of those stairs!

I spent the next hour busily packing luggage full of me and the girls' clothes while Ruby helped by haphazardly throwing random toys and clothes into her little suitcase. Daisy was content to watch us, giggling the whole time. About the time I was ready to take a break, I noticed Ruby had stopped packing, and her little eyes were focused on the doorway behind me. That's when I sensed that someone else was in the room, and when I felt them grab me, I thought my heart was going to jump out of my chest. As I struggled to break free of their grip, I heard a voice that nearly brought me to tears.

"Where are you going, querida?"

I spun around and was face to face with the most handsome man in Rio and Houston. A peace fell over me as I smiled at him. In the weeks since I'd seen him, he'd grown a beard, which seemed to add to his handsomeness. I rubbed my fingers over the coarse hair on his face.

"What are you doing here?" I asked.

"You called. I came," he answered, then leaned in and kissed me softly on the lips.

"How did you get in? What are you doing in Houston? How long have you been here?"

"I still have a key. Remember, you changed the locks and gave me a key before I left. You never took it from me. And I never left Houston."

"I… I thought you went back to Rio."

"I was going to leave. I went to the airport, got an earlier flight, but I did not want to go back without my family. So I stayed in a hotel, and I waited."

I hugged him tightly, so very relieved to be able to wrap my arms around him again. "You waited? What if I'd never called you and said I wanted to try again."

"I knew you would call."

"Now, how did you know that?"

"Because you love me. Heart to heart, remember?"

I smiled as I rested my head against his chest. "I do love you. I love you with all my heart, Victor."

"I know. And I love you, querida."

Remembering my pastor's words, I said, "Victor, I need to ask you something."

"Yes?"

"Are you saved? I mean, have you accepted Jesus as your savior?"

He frowned slightly. "I believe I have. As a boy."

I grasped both of his hands. "Let's not take any chances on this. Will you repeat after me?"

"Wait, do you think God will forgive me for what I was?"

"If you ask Him, I know He will."

"Do you forgive me?"

I smiled. "I forgave you the moment I fell in love with you, Victor."

He returned my smile and nodded. "Okay, let's do this."

As we recited the sinner's prayer together, Ruby hugged her

daddy's leg and smiled. Daisy cooed and giggled in the background, and in my heart, I thanked God over and over again for my family.

"Victor, are you ready?!" I shouted as I hung up the phone and pulled my shoes on. "We've got to leave in enough time to drop the kids off at your mother's house!"

"I know, querida. There's enough time. Just calm down." He walked into our bedroom dressed in a white suit, looking like he'd just stepped out of a men's fashion magazine. After all those years of marriage, the man still made me take pause. I sat there at the foot of our bed and stared at him. I could do nothing else. "Who were you on the phone with?" he asked.

"My mom."

He smiled as he leaned over and kissed me. "I am glad you two are talking more often."

I nodded. "Me, too. She wants us to visit soon. I told her I'd think about it."

"Good." He eyed me for a moment and said, "Do we have to go to that place tonight? I would rather stay here and take that beautiful dress off of you."

I grinned. "I'd like that, too. But we can't miss this event. I still can't believe the company is throwing the book launch party here in São Paulo. The last time, we had to fly back to the states."

He shrugged as he sat down beside me and rested his hand on my thigh. He reached behind me and grabbed our latest book from the bed. He held it up and said, "Well, the book is set here in Brazil. I guess they thought it would be appropriate to celebrate here."

I gazed at the book in his hand and silently read the words on the cover: *The Diva and the Gigolo by Alexandria Weaver-Castro and Victor Castro.* The blurb read, "Fiction's hottest husband and wife duo have done it again!"

As Victor stared down at the book, I said, "I wonder if anyone would believe how much of that is the truth."

He smiled as he shifted his focus to my face. "*Used* to be true. I am no longer a gigolo, remember?"

I pursed my lips. "You better not be."

"Ah, querida." He leaned in and gave me one of those Brazilian kisses of his, and before I realized it, we were lying in the bed, tugging on each other's clothes. *I guess we're gonna be late*, I thought. But before we could really get anything started, the pitter patter of little feet shook us apart. We'd forgotten just that quickly that it was early evening and the kids were home and awake. Three little amber-eyed girls and one little boy ran into our room, giggling and grinning as they jumped into the bed between me and Victor. Ruby, Daisy, Pearl, and Victor Jr. all pounced on their father at once. It took a good ten minutes to pry them all off of him so that we could leave. As we piled into our SUV, Victor said, "I'll finish what we started later tonight."

I smiled, remembering that the kids were spending the night with his mother. "I look forward to it," I said.

He reached for my hand and squeezed it in his. "I love you, minha querida."

"I love you, too."

Bonus (Soundtrack) Track:

"Gigolos Get Lonely Too" *The Time*

To learn more about anger management, visit:
http://www.apa.org/topics/anger/control.aspx

To learn more about help available for adult victims of child abuse,
visit: http://www.havoca.org/

To learn more about Author Adrienne Thompson, visit,
http://adriennethompsonwrites.webs.com

Sign up for Adrienne's newsletter here: http://eepurl.com/jnDmH

Follow Adrienne on Twitter!

https://twitter.com/A_H_Thompson

Like Adrienne on Facebook!

https://www.facebook.com/AdrienneThompsonWrites

Follow Adrienne on Pinterest!

http://www.pinterest.com/ahthompsn/

Also by Adrienne Thompson:

The *Bluesday* Series:

Bluesday

Lovely Blues

Blues In The Key Of B

Locked out of Heaven (Tomeka's Story – A Bluesday Continuation)

The *Been So Long* Series:

Rapture (A Been So Long Prequel)

If (Wasif's Story) A Been So Long Prequel

Been So Long

Little Sister (Cleo's Story—a companion novel to Been So Long)

Been So Long 2 (Body and Soul)

Been So Long III (Whatever It Takes)

The *Your Love Is King* Series

Your Love Is King

Better

Stand-alone novels:

See Me

When You've Been Blessed (Feels Like Heaven)

Nonfiction Titles:

Just Between Us (Inspiring Stories by Women) –as a contributor

Seven Days of Change (A Flash Devotional)

All books are available at <u>amazon.com</u>, <u>barnesandnoble.com</u>, and <u>kobobooks.com</u>

Excerpt from Home

(Coming Spring 2015)

I sat behind my huge desk and tried to keep my concentration while I rattled off a letter to Alma, my new secretary. Alma Lopez was half-Puerto Rican and half-Haitian. She was also young and attractive, and she knew it. Every other minute, she flipped her long, black hair over her shoulder or re-crossed her long, shapely legs, letting her short skirt ride up higher and higher. I shifted in my seat and told myself to stop looking at her. I knew women like Alma. They used sex to get what they wanted, and they usually succeeded. In the past, they'd *always* succeeded with me.

For years, I was an open book when it came to women. If you were young and attractive, you could easily get me. Woman after woman, night after night, and I seemed to be powerless to change. I loved women, no, let me correct that. I *love* women. The way they smell, the way they walk, their lips, *everything*. I've been powerless to resist a beautiful woman for years. But, I'm proud to say that I hadn't given in to my weakness in weeks. I know that doesn't sound like much of an accomplishment, but for me it really was. I woke up one morning beside a lovely lady and decided I was tired of the flavor-of-the-night lifestyle I'd been living. Maybe it was time for me to settle down. Or maybe I was just tired.

I finished dictating a letter to Alma and smiled at her. "Okay, thanks, Alma. Be sure to have that letter ready by the morning."

She smiled seductively, or maybe that's just how it seemed to me. "Yes, sir. Um, Mr. Spencer? Can I ask you a question?"

I nodded. "Sure."

"Is it true that you were a rapper back in the day?"

Oh, that. Fame was like crack to women like Alma, even if it was faded fame. They'd do anything to get close to it. "Um, yes. But that was years ago," I said.

She lit up like a Pentecostal church. "Wow! When I got this job, my cousin told me you used to be Masta T.I.P., but I thought she was crazy. Then I looked on the internet, and I saw the pictures. I saw that it was you. This is great! I've never met a real live star before. Well, there was that time I saw Usher at a club, but I didn't get close to him."

I shrugged. "Well, I'd hardly call myself a star. I haven't performed in years. Real estate is my thing now."

"Yeah, uh-huh. Do you still have any pictures, or anything from back in the day?" Alma wasn't paying a bit of attention to what I was saying.

"Alma, I don't think that'd be a good idea. Like I said, that was years ago. If you don't mind, I have some phone calls to make."

Her face fell. "Oh, okay." She left my office, closing the door behind her. I watched through the frosted glass of the door as she settled behind her own desk and dialed a number on her cell phone.

My letter was forgotten as she engaged in a lively phone conversation.

I sighed. More than twenty years had passed, and Masta T.I.P. was still coming back to haunt me. But I suppose I couldn't expect to ever be able to totally shake that part of my life. I was a pretty successful rapper in the nineties. I made a lot of money and bedded a lot of women. Most men would've been glad to relive those glory days, but honestly, I was kind of ashamed of that period of my life. I owned a successful real estate agency despite the state of the economy. I was a respectable business man, and I wanted to be known for that, not a long-lost rap career. Hell, I didn't even listen to rap anymore. Give me a good John Legend CD any day.

I grabbed my cell phone and clipped it to my belt, shoved a few papers into my briefcase, and headed out of my office. As I stepped into the reception area, I stopped dead in my tracks. Alma was bent over, picking something up from the floor, and I had a full view of her butt. I loosened my tie and cleared my throat. "I'm heading out, Alma," I said.

She stood up straight and turned to look at me with a smile on her face. "Oh, okay. I'll lock up."

I nodded and headed toward the door. I started to open it and then stopped and turned around. "Um, Alma. If you'd like, you can come over to my house and have dinner with me tonight. I have a couple of photo albums full of pictures from back in the day. You can look to your heart's content."

She lit up again. "Really?!"

"Sure. What's your address? I'll pick you up around seven."

I never said I was perfect. I was still a work in progress, and Alma Lopez was too fine to miss out on.